INSPIRED BY THE
NETFLIX ORIGINAL SERIES

LOST
IN
SPACE®

Little, Brown and Company
Hachette Book Group
1290 Avenue of the Americas, New York, NY 10104
Visit us at LBYR.com

First Edition: May 2020

Little, Brown and Company is a division of Hachette Book Group, Inc.
The Little, Brown name and logo are trademarks of Hachette Book Group, Inc.

The publisher is not responsible for websites (or their content) that are not owned by the publisher.

LCCN: 2020932858

ISBNs: 978-0-316-42597-1 (paper over board), 978-0-316-42598-8 (ebook)

Printed in the United States of America

LSC-C

10 9 8 7 6 5 4 3 2 1

INSPIRED BY THE
NETFLIX ORIGINAL SERIES

LOST IN SPACE®

Infinity's Edge

An original novel by
Kevin Emerson

LITTLE, BROWN AND COMPANY
New York   Boston

Special thanks to
Synthesis Entertainment

Prologue

Mission Log 87
Robinson, Maureen—Commander
24th Mission of the Resolute

Good morning. I know I've been recording fewer logs lately but, well, after six months, there isn't much new to report. We're learning more and more every day about this water planet that we're stranded on...but we still don't know how to get off it.

There's been no contact with the Resolute, as usual. They could be to Alpha Centauri and back by now, assuming they were able to find their way back on course from our last planet. For us, this sector that we've found ourselves in is even more unfamiliar than the one we left. It's cloudy most nights here, but when I do get a view of the stars, I can't make any sense of them. It's safe to say we're more lost than ever.

But chin up, right, Maureen? There have been some positive developments in the last couple of weeks. John's crops have started to yield food—he's so proud—and I have to admit, eating real corn and tomatoes is a welcome break from rehydrated meal packs. The greenhouse's hydroponics systems are working well. The only real problem is the wind damage to the plastic walls. The poisonous atmosphere here is just as lethal for the plants as it is for us. So far, we've been able to keep on top of patching any holes, but we have to stay vigilant.

Same with the solar panels. As long as we can keep the sand from building up on them, they are providing enough power for the oxygen-generating system as well as for our suits. However, that's barely enough energy even on the brightest day, and there's never any leftover to store in the Jupiter's batteries. And of course, we still have yet to find a way to use the methane in this atmosphere for rocket fuel, which we'll need a lot of if we're going to take off.

Another week, another month…I'm still studying

that strange occurrence of lightning storms out on the horizon. They happen like clockwork every twenty-three days. I can't help but think that those storms could be the key to us leaving here if I could just figure out how to harness their power.

In the meantime, everyone's doing all right. Penny and Judy are fine. John's a happy farmer—to be honest, I think he wishes we'd stay here. Don is Don, and Smith is…well, I shouldn't say what I think she is.…

But I'm still worried about Will. Most of the time he seems fine; he says he's fine, but these days that's about all he ever says. I know he still misses the Robot. I keep thinking enough time will pass and he'll get over it, but I fear he's getting worse: more solitary, more withdrawn. I see everybody trying to bond with him, but he just won't come out of his shell. Granted, there isn't much for him to do here, which makes it worse. He spends so many hours off alone, exploring our little island world. Maybe if he had someone his own age around, a friend…I should go exploring with him sometime. But there's so much more I need to study.

Ugh.

I guess that's it for now. I should focus on the positive: We're as healthy and safe as a family stranded on an uncharted planet can be. Back to work on those lightning storms. I'll update again in a few days....

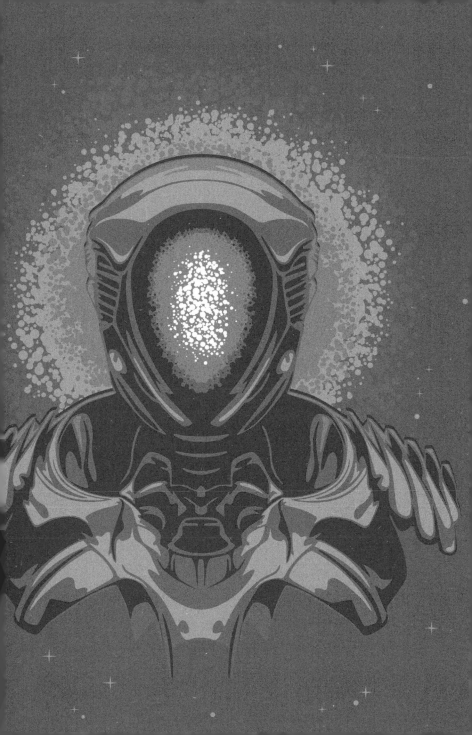

TWO DAYS BEFORE LOWEST TIDE

CHAPTER

1

My name is Will Robinson, and I'm in danger.
Danger of complete boredom.

I mean, okay, sure, there's still real danger; we're stranded on a little sand island on a poison water planet. We're always one bad windstorm from losing our solar cells and our garden, which would also mean losing our air and our food. We have no fuel to take off and no idea where the *Resolute* or anyone else in the 24th colonist group is. We don't even know where *we* are.

But all that being said, while I do have a list of daily jobs, like testing the hydroponics chemistry in our garden and checking the underside of the

Jupiter for corrosion, there's not very much to do here.

Especially when you don't have any friends.

I know, I have Judy and Penny, Mom and Dad, and Don. Dr. Smith is here, too, but she's under house arrest in an air lock, and I try to avoid even walking by her door. The rest of us have fun now and then, but it's not the same.

I miss him. My Robot. Whenever I think back to exploring our old planet with him, tromping through the forest, clapping for the flowers, avoiding mothasaurs, even discovering the occasional time-portal-in-a-cave...I can't stand the feeling it gives me: the stinging in my eyes, the tightness in my chest. Have you ever felt like someone saw the world the exact same way you did? Like you had the same brain? And have you ever had to say goodbye to that person as they tumbled out of an air lock while fighting an enemy robot?

Okay, probably not that last part, but what about the rest of it? I'd never felt like that about a friend before, and I haven't since—

Except for Clare.

But I shouldn't talk about her. I mean, she wasn't even...

Was she my friend? I guess that depends. Sort of like with the Robot: Sometimes I wondered if he was just following a program because I saved his life, or if he actually liked, you know, *me*. Could he even make a friend? Did he have a concept of what that was? I'm not sure, but I guess no matter how much you think about something, at some point you have to decide if you're going to believe it or not. I believed in the Robot, and I believed in Clare; I think I still do, even if what happened nearly got me and my entire family killed.

As you can probably guess, they don't know about that.

If the Robot had been around, he never would have let it happen. But he wasn't there, and so the day I met Clare started like every other day here, with the sound of Dad's voice speaking quietly:

"Hey, rise and shine, Farmer Will."

My eyes blinked open, and I saw Dad's silhouette

in the doorway of my compartment. I checked the time: almost six. Time to do the plant chemistry before the sun came up, just like every other day.

"Be right there," I croaked.

Dad tapped the side of the door and headed down to the cargo bay.

For a second, I shivered and pulled up my blanket. The hull of the ship creaked, and I heard the steady howling of the wind. Every day here is windy; it's just a question of how strong the wind will be. That morning sounded about medium, which meant you had to lean into it when you walked around, but at least it wasn't going to try to nick your suit or tear your greenhouse apart.

But then I bolted up because I remembered that it was an important day: one of the three lowest tides of the entire time we'd been here. Mom and I had been keeping track of the tides, because how much the water level changes, especially how much it rises, has a pretty big impact on whether we'll still have a place to live. We'd learned that this planet has diurnal tides just like on Earth, including the more drastic spring tides, but here they aren't nearly as regular. Every four or five months, there are these super-extreme tides, where the higher ones are much higher and the lower ones are much lower. It has something to do with this place having two moons instead of one. There had been a set of these extreme tides not long after we'd arrived, and if our calculations were right, there was going to be another set over the next few days. That meant our island was going to shrink down pretty far during the high tides—we'd even dug trenches around the greenhouse just to be safe—and the low tides would be prime time for exploring.

As I swung my legs over the side of my bed, a familiar shape caught the corner of my eye: the silhouette of the Robot—not *really* him, just a little model I'd made on our old planet. Yet every time I saw it I felt this little tug inside, a squeeze of energy like, *Is it him?* Then I immediately felt stupid because of course it wasn't.

"Where are you?" I said quietly. Sometimes I thought if I concentrated really hard, I might be able to picture where the Robot was, might even be able to see what he was seeing—we'd had a connection like that, once upon a time—but it never quite worked. Maybe he was still tumbling through space, locked in battle with that other robot, the one we called SAR. Maybe their joints had frozen up by now and they would just drift that way, forever.

"You'd like exploring these low tides today," I said to the model, and then, swallowing hard, I turned away and grabbed my space suit from the floor.

I stood and tugged it on, wiggling my feet in my boots, trying to make as much room as I could. Just because you were lost in space didn't mean you stopped growing, but it *did* mean that you couldn't get the next size bigger suit, and mine had gotten pretty constricting over the last six months.

As I struggled to zip the suit up to my collar, I felt what had become a familiar sensation on the back of my neck: a burning feeling that made me immediately start scratching there, even though Judy had told me not to. The spot had started to itch two days earlier. The skin was red, and even though it didn't itch all the time, the flare-ups had gotten more frequent and more intense. At first, Judy had thought it was some sort of rash, maybe from my suit chafing—it *was* stretched pretty tight—but we'd tried putting a bandage there and it hadn't helped. Her next theory was that it was some kind of allergic reaction, except so far, she hadn't been able to figure out what I might be allergic to. She'd run the standard set of tests on me, and while I had tested mildly positive for an allergy to silicates, which we'd detected in the sand and rock formations on this planet, it shouldn't have been enough to cause this kind of reaction.

We're in an exotic atmosphere and habitat, Judy had said. *We have control of our climate and food, but we can't be one-hundred-percent sure what particles in this world we might be exposed to.* For the moment, the treatment she'd prescribed was to wear an antihistamine patch on my wrist and just try not to scratch. Wearing my suit was actually helpful since it kept my fingers off my neck.

Once I was suited up, I walked as quietly as I could down the curving hall of the *Jupiter*, past the doors to the other sleeping compartments. The ship was dark except for the dim outside light that was coming through the cockpit windows and the skylights in the hub. Both rooms were empty, but the hall smelled like coffee, so I knew Mom was up already—she always was—which also meant I knew where she was.

Dad was waiting for me down in the cargo bay. He had his helmet under one arm. In the other hand he held a hurricane lamp, its flame burning blue. I took my breathing pack from its charging station on the wall, slung it over my shoulders, and pulled my helmet from its hook.

"Ready?" Dad was smiling at me as if it wasn't a drag to be up this early.

"Yup." I put my helmet under my arm and got the probe from its charger.

We walked down the open ramp of the cargo bay, our boots clomping, then through a short, round tunnel made of plastic and into the domed greenhouse. The air was warmer here, with a sweet, damp smell. Water droplets beaded on the plastic surface, which was stretched over a skeleton of thin metal poles. Dad said it reminded him of camping when he was a kid.

All around us were our crops: corn, cherry tomatoes, soybeans, carrots; some of the nymph oranges were finally starting to bear tiny fruits. Everything grew out of vessels of water, the stems and leaves climbing around supports that stretched from the floor to the ceiling. Dad had said that none of these plants looked exactly like they would have back on Earth; everything had been genetically designed to grow quicker and smaller and without soil. We'd never been able to have a garden at our house because of the bad air and the water shortages, which was maybe why I'd never really been interested in gardening, but it was kinda cool to have all this food around you that you actually grew. Maybe this was a tiny bit like having a pet? One that just sort of stood there all the time, but still.... Also, I had to admit, it did make us pretty rugged explorers to be able to grow our own food on an uncharted planet.

Dad breathed in deeply. "Another day living off the land." He waved a meter in front of him. "Oxygen mix is right," he reported. "Methane leakage is holding steady below three parts per million."

I stepped into the narrow gap between the corn plants. Here, closer to the greenhouse wall, you could hear the wind whipping outside and the hiss of sand grains and pebbles striking the plastic, which was dotted with patches. I knelt down and pushed the sleek metal end of the probe into one of the water vessels, which was almost completely filled by a ball of roots. The results appeared on my wrist communicator.

As I knelt, a wave of burning itchiness radiated from my neck. I moved my gloved fingers there, but with my suit on it was no use. I took a deep breath and tried to relax.

"You okay over there?" Dad called.

"Yeah, fine, just my allergy thing," I said.

"Is it worse?"

"About the same."

"Well, make sure you check in with Judy again today."

"Yeah, okay." I stood. The flare-up was passing. "The pH is looking good," I reported, and moved along to check the beans. "Nitrogen and phosphorus are holding steady…just the potassium is low again."

"Like clockwork," said Dad. He was rubbing a cotton swab between the flowers of the nymph orange plants. "Looks like we might not have oranges in time to put them in our stockings after all."

"Huh?"

He shook his head. "Nothing; weird old Christmas tradition. Like, from *my* great-grandparents. But"—he surveyed the rest of the crops—"it does seem like we really can have a decent Thanksgiving next week, especially if Don lets us at that chicken of his." My head whipped around to Dad, but he was grinning. "I'm just kidding. How are the rest of the readings?"

"Fine," I said, moving on to the tomatoes. "Just the potassium. I'll update the irrigation settings."

"Perfect." Dad held up a wand-like scanner and began waving it around the sides of the greenhouse; it used sonic waves to check for weak points in the plastic so we could stay ahead of any tears. When the scanner started to beep, Dad made an X on the plastic with a marker.

I moved to the control station by the entrance to adjust the irrigation settings, then met up with Dad by the air lock on the far side of the greenhouse.

"Let's go," he said.

We clamped our helmets into place and stepped through to the outside.

The wind shoved us like a schoolyard bully as our feet mushed into the gray sand. There was a hiss as sand sprayed against our visors. All around us was a watery gray world: layers of waves and clouds, the flash of whitecaps, and here and there the black teeth of rocks that stuck out of the sand, some only a meter or two, but others that towered above us. Our *Jupiter* was parked on an oval-shaped sand island. When the tides were high, it looked like a lonely little dot surrounded by ocean, but when they were low, other islands appeared, as if our spot was part of a chain of islands, or at least a brief sandbar.

During the lowest tides, you could follow the island chain quite a ways, like playing an ocean version of hopscotch. The shapes of the islands were always changing as the waves eroded and deposited sand. Sometimes, the bridge between two islands would disappear for a week or two, or a new rock would get uncovered, or a whole new little landform would show up, only to erode away a couple of days later.

Not too far from the *Jupiter* was a formation of rocks that made a little jagged bluff. Beside that was Mom's small work hut, a light glowing inside. She'd probably already been in there for an hour or two.

Dad and I were rounding the side of the greenhouse when a line of light appeared on the horizon. For just a moment, the planet's fused twin suns—technically contact binary stars—appeared, reflecting brightly on our helmet visors and making us squint. Everything lit up in orange and gold, and you could feel the warmth through your suit. I stopped and watched, getting green dots in my eyes, before the suns disappeared into the upper cloud layers and the light got flat and gray again. That was often the only time we'd see them all day.

I ducked under the *Jupiter* to start my next job, checking the hull for evidence of corrosion, while Dad examined each of the landing struts for the same thing, peering into their hydraulics with his headlamp.

I walked back and forth, being careful to check every panel for the little indentations that were the first sign of corrosion. Streaks of rust came next, and they were evidence that the toxic air and water had eaten through the panels' protective coating and started to affect the metal. That had only happened in one place, but we'd had to patch it immediately because our life support had started to leak out while the toxic outside air started getting in. This was the prime suspect on Judy's list of causes for my allergic reaction. Damaged panels would also be a problem if we were ever going to launch off this planet, because we'd need the thermal shielding to work. Not to mention, if this water started to get up into the *Jupiter*'s internal systems, it could cripple them entirely.

So I examined the panels meter by meter, trying to pay close attention and not let my mind wander, because while it was important work, it wasn't exactly interesting. When I reached the area we'd patched, I turned on my helmet lights and used my scanner to check the metal integrity. So far, it was holding strong.

By the time I was finished and walking back around the greenhouse, Don and Judy were outside, using long brushes to clean off the solar panel array.

"Everything looks good," I reported to Dad.

"Nice work," he said, patting my shoulder.

We returned to the cargo bay and pulled off our helmets.

"Want some breakfast?" Dad asked.

"Oh, that's okay." I tapped my communicator. "This morning is the third-lowest spring tide. I was going to explore."

"Oh, right." Dad nodded to himself. "You and your mom have been tracking those." I could tell he was trying to think of something to say to me, just like I'd seen everyone doing lately. "Did you already eat?"

I stepped past him, walking quickly to the ladder. "I've got snacks in my pack."

"Well, be back by midday, then. All right?"

I smiled as best I could. "Sure." If the Robot had been around, Dad probably would have been fine letting me go out and explore all day, but without him I was just little Will, who was too young and fragile.

I hurried to my compartment, got my pack, and slung it over my shoulders. I heard Dad's voice in the cockpit and slipped by, heading back to the cargo bay.

"Where you off to, halfling?" Penny was sitting on a couch in the hub, knees up, writing in her journal.

"Low tide," I said.

"Cool," she said absently, her pen scratching along.

I almost added, *Wanna come?* Having Penny along was a little like being with the Robot, because she was always off in her own head and didn't really respond when I said stuff to her, except most of the time it didn't seem like she was actually listening. We'd had fun naming islands or studying tide pools, but she rarely wanted to go out. "How's the journal coming?" I asked instead.

"Memoir," she said. "Like a journal, but *literary*."

"Oh."

Penny got a gleam in her eye and spoke in a dramatic voice: "I'm at the part where you're falling into space, doomed to die, before Dad rescues you."

"Great," I said. There it was again in my head: the memory of my hands slipping from the ladder on the outside of the *Jupiter*, of falling, sure that I was doomed, my arms and legs flailing helplessly, the ship shrinking. Thinking of it made my upper arm ache; I had a wound there that hadn't quite healed.

"Hey." Penny was peering at me. "Don't worry, I'm making sure to point out how brave you were to climb out there and close the air lock. Readers will know that you saved our lives—"

"Before I needed saving," I muttered, turning and walking out.

"Hey, Will!" Penny called after me. Except I knew she wouldn't come after me; she'd just get back to her writing. Which was how I wanted it… I think… whatever. I just wanted to get going.

Back outside in the whipping wind and damp, chilly air, I trudged across the hard sand, away from the greenhouse.

Judy and Don were still by the solar panels. They were gesturing avidly to each other, so I switched channels on my communicator until their voices popped into my helmet.

"And *I'm* telling *you* that these panels need to be recalibrated," Judy was saying.

"That *might* be true," said Don, glancing up

at the clouds, "*if* there was any sunlight for calibrating. I doubt the tide was really that high last night. I don't remember hearing anything shifting around."

"With your snoring, you wouldn't know if there had been a hurricane."

"I—" Don paused, noticing me, and waved in my direction. "Morning, chief."

I just waved as if I wasn't hearing him and kept walking.

Judy waved her arms more emphatically, and I stopped. "Hey!" she called. "How's the allergy today?"

"It's the same, I think." Just talking about it made my neck itch.

"Is it presenting in any new locations?"

"Presenting?"

"She means are you itchy anywhere else," said Don.

"No. It's just like it was." I didn't add *I think*, because if I'd wanted to be honest I might have said that the rash *did* feel a little more intense and burny today than it had yesterday, but saying that would fully activate Dr. Judy, and I'd lose my low tide exploring time to yet another exam. "I'll be back by lunch."

"Okay, be careful," said Judy.

I nodded and trudged on, past where the chariot was parked, and skirted around the edge of the rocky bluff and Mom's work hut. Most of the time, the water came right up and sloshed against the rocks, but this morning's low tide meant there was a strip of sand a few meters wide between the rocks and the water. The sand was almost completely dry, scribbled with a line of dried-out, crusty kelp—the kind that, when wet, glowed with a blue-green bioluminescence.

I had just gotten to the other side of the bluff when my communicator buzzed.

"Morning," said Mom, sounding cheery. I looked back and saw her peering between the plastic walls of her hut—we actually referred to it as *the office*, as in, every morning when Mom left, she said, *I'm heading out to the office.*

I smiled at her, but also sighed to myself. "Hey."

"Off exploring on the spring tides?"

I nodded.

"Aren't you proud? Our tide chart calculations were correct."

"Yup." I knew that Mom thought our charts were a way to bond with me—we had ones of the moon phases and seasons, too—and that she thought the bonding was important, because she was worried about me. She knew that losing the Robot had been hard for me.

When I thought about that, though, it actually made me feel kinda frustrated. It might have been nice if she'd tried to see how important the Robot had been while he was still around.

Neither of us said anything for a moment. The wind whipped against my helmet.

"Okay," Mom finally said, "well, just—"

"Be back around lunchtime," I finished for her. "Yeah, I know."

"Of course you do," Mom said to herself. "Um…"

I almost wanted to tell her that I could hear her

worrying about me every time she tried to choose her words so carefully. It made me want to shout, *Just stop trying!*

"I'll be careful, and I'll have a good time," I said, beating her to it, and I turned and started across the sand.

"Have fun!" Mom called after me. That didn't help, either.

As I walked away, this dark anger brewed inside me. Why couldn't everyone just stop worrying? None of them had really wanted the Robot around when he had been here, and it made their worry now seem fake.

Besides, I'm fine, I thought as I walked away. *I can handle everything on my own.*

I had no idea how wrong I was about to be.

CHAPTER

2

I reached the edge of our island and paused. When the tide was low, there were three more islands in our chain. Penny and I had named the next one the Whaleback, because it was just a basic oval hump sticking out of the water. This was the only one that was actually still visible at high tide, but you had to wade through about twenty meters of water to get to it. Even though our space suits could protect us from the toxic atmosphere here, they wouldn't last long submerged in that water. This morning, though, you could easily cross to the Whaleback. In fact, the water level was so low that the Whaleback looked like a small hill.

I jogged across the soft sandbar connector and scrambled up to the top. From here, you could see back across our island, which ended at deep water not far past the *Jupiter*. Beyond that there was open ocean basically in all directions.

The next island after the Whaleback wasn't exactly an island; it looked more like a bunch of weathered rocks that poked out of the sand, with tide pools in between them. We had very creatively named this one the Pools, and it only appeared when the tides were low. This was Penny's favorite spot to come and hang out. She liked looking at the little snaillike creatures that you could sometimes find. They had cool bioluminescent colors on the edges of their shells, like the kelp.

You had to balance carefully and hop over the tide pools to reach the third and final island: the Serpent. This one was *my* favorite. It started as a long, skinny sand ridge that, as you probably guessed, curved back and forth in an S shape like the body of a snake. Then, almost fifty meters later, it rose up to this broad, diamond-shaped rock made of a smooth black volcanic mineral that really did look like it might be the head of some giant creature.

The Serpent's head ended at a short cliff that dropped into the waves. If you climbed a little way over the edge, there was a ledge where you could sit and be completely out of sight from the *Jupiter,* even from Mom's office. So you could just be there and think your thoughts without worrying that somebody was watching you and wondering what was on your mind and if you were okay and blah blah blah.

Except—

As I peered ahead, I saw that today, the Serpent's head didn't seem to be the end of the island chain. With the flat gray sky and the wind and the constant ocean mist, it was hard to be sure, but it looked like there was something else out there. The spring tide had revealed a new island!

My pulse ticked up and a burst of excitement ran through me. You're probably thinking that finding sandbar islands is kind of a dumb thing to be getting all excited about, but you have to remember that finding little sandbar islands is pretty much *all* there is to do here, except for sitting around thinking about all the things you *can't* do.

I bounded down the Whaleback and hopped my way across the Pools. Out of the corner of my eye I saw little flashes of color; with the low tide, there were quite a few snails near the surface. It made me wonder if there might also be one of those spiny, starfish-like creatures out hunting them. Penny and I had only seen one of those a couple of months earlier, and we had been looking for another ever since. But that could wait.

You might think that finding sea-creature life on another planet would be pretty amazing, but let me tell you, when there's no one else around to share your discovery with except for your family, and when the creatures' methane chemistry makes them totally toxic to eat, they get boring pretty fast. Also, there didn't seem to be any larger creatures in this ocean. Don had tried fishing a couple of times—not that we would have been able to eat anything he caught—but hadn't had any luck. Even seeing some sort of fish or whales or anything in the distance would have been neat.

I leaped from the last rock of the Pools to the narrow, twisting back of the Serpent and then followed its S curves back and forth. Even with the tide as low as it was, if I strayed off the meter-wide hump, my footprints filled with puddles the minute I lifted my boot.

I was breathing hard by the time I reached the Serpent's head. I scrambled up its slick, damp side and stood perched at the edge of the small cliff that dropped to the water, the spot that, on every other trip out here, had been the end of the line.

But not today. Sure enough, across a meter or two of deep water, a pointy black rock jutted into the air. Beyond that was a long, skinny sandbar, just barely above the waves lapping at its sides. This new shallow bar shot away from me in an almost impossibly straight line, probably a hundred meters long, until it finally ended in the distance at a triangle-shaped rock sticking out of the sand, like a finger pointed at the sky.

I tapped my communicator to activate the camera on my helmet, and zoomed in on that distant rock. Actually, it looked more like three rocks clustered together, wider at their bases and skinnier at the tops, with a sort of pyramidal shape, like three large, narrow triangles angling to the same point. There was a shadow between them, like maybe the rocks surrounded a cool little spot to hide out and be protected from the wind. I looked back over my shoulder, at the distant *Jupiter* and Mom's office. That new spot was nice and far from worried eyes, too.

I looked at the new sandbar leading to the rocks and checked my communicator again: From our calculations, I had about an hour before the tide would bottom out and start to come back in. How long would this bar stay above water after that? I figured I had time, as long as I was quick.

Step one was to get across this channel of deep water below me. I opened the Exploration tool on my communicator. It had a laser measurement device, which I aimed at that rock on the other side of the channel. The laser flashed and calculated the distance: 2.2 meters. I tapped a little JUMP symbol beside the results. A graphic of me and a curving line to the rock appeared. The Exploration tool was loaded with physical activity data from tests we'd done back on Earth and on the *Resolute*, and it used that plus the gravity here, the weight of my suit, and my current biometrics to calculate results: JUMP DIFFICULTY: SLIGHTLY ABOVE AVERAGE. CHANCE OF SUCCESS: 67%.

Those weren't exactly great odds. Two out of three times I would make it, but every third time I'd fall into deadly water....This would have been a pretty good time to have a large, super-strong Robot around. I pictured him lifting me in his strong metal arms and then bounding easily across with a burst of his servos, his feet crunching onto the rock on the other side—*Stop thinking about that,* I told myself, swallowing hard. *Gotta do things on your own, Will Robinson.* Besides, those odds did say I was more likely to make it than not.

I climbed down to the ledge on the back side of the Serpent's head. I checked behind me, confirming to myself that I was invisible to Mom or anyone else who might be looking for me...then I held my breath and jumped.

I made it—well, almost. My right foot landed on the slippery, still-wet part of the rock and plunged into the water up to my knee. I grabbed at the slick edges of the rock and managed to get a tight grip with my fingers before I fell any farther. Heart racing, breathing hard, I pulled myself up and clambered to the pointy top to sit and check my suit for leaks. A tear when I was this far from the *Jupiter* could be a real problem, but everything looked all right and my suit levels were normal.

I sat there for a second, catching my breath, then I scrambled off the rock and started across the narrow sandbar. It was almost like walking on a balance beam. I trudged along the wet sand, keeping my steps close together, but still going as fast as possible. I could *not* risk being out here when the tide shifted.

The triangle rock formation was getting closer. It was darker than the other rocks of the island chain, and unlike those others, which had jagged surfaces, these rocks were pretty smooth, like they'd been eroded over time. As I approached, I saw that the rocks were about chest high. Not that big, but still…I looked behind me and wondered: How had I not seen these before? They seemed tall enough that they would have been sticking out of the water during other low tides, but maybe with their narrow tops, they hadn't made much of an impression amid all the waves.

My neck flared up, the burning sensation increasing, and I instinctually tried to scratch there, but of course it didn't do any good through my suit. I was sweating now from this long walk in heavy sand, which was probably setting it off. I tapped my communicator and lowered my suit temperature.

In another couple of minutes I reached the triangle rocks. I stepped around the nearest one, running my hand over the surface. It was smooth like it had appeared from a distance, but now I could see that it was covered with little pit marks, like tiny, round gouges. And there were little grayish stripes bleeding down from each of the pits. The streaks were dry beneath my gloves, but they reminded me of the corrosion that I had to watch for beneath the *Jupiter*. I hadn't seen any other rocks with these kinds of markings, but then again I'd explored approximately point-zero-zero-zero-zero-one percent of this planet, so there had to be all kinds of different geology besides just what was right on our island.

I opened the scanner on my communicator and aimed it at the rock. The screen pulsed for a minute, then flashed: UNKNOWN MATERIAL. That was nothing new; it said that about everything in this place. Below that was a list of the material's components, and while nearly 50 percent of it was an *unknown composite*, the rest of it was made of elements with familiar names: titanium, iron, and silica, which were basic universal building blocks. There was something comforting about that.

I peered into the gap between the three rock columns. Like I'd thought, there was a space about a meter wide that extended down below the sand I was standing on. The bottom was sloped with sand, with a puddle on one half. I stepped down inside, and immediately the sound of the wind died away. Its constant push on my body, the hiss against my visor and suit—it all quieted down. I was surprised how relaxed it made me feel, how my shoulders loosened up. I ducked, and the effect was even more pronounced. The sounds of my movements echoed off the rock walls around me. Almost peaceful—

"Ow!" I felt the sharp poke on the back of my leg and flinched away. There was something pointy sticking out from one of the rocks, but first I checked my communicator. If I'd gotten a suit tear... But there was no alert, no flashing warnings. I sighed with relief. *Gotta be more careful!* I thought angrily. *No Robot here to warn you when there's danger...*

And yet, even the Robot probably wouldn't have noticed this. I bent down and examined the base of the rock. The pointy thing was actually a shell. It was a dark gray to camouflage with the rocks but had those light blue edges that we'd seen on other shells, which would make it glow at night. The shell shape was like the others we'd seen, which most resembled the common periwinkle snail back on Earth—but this one was larger and pointier, maybe a different subspecies, which meant Mom and Judy would definitely want to see it. I pinched at it and pulled, and it popped free with a dry crunching sound. That was a clue for what I found when I turned it over: The inside of the shell was empty. So much for finding a new life form.

"You almost killed me," I said to it, and I nearly tossed it out in the water, but I noticed that the inner walls of the spiral shell were shiny with purple and orange iridescent patches. It was worth adding to my collection back on the *Jupiter.* I opened a water-proof pocket on my belt and dropped the shell in.

Another wave of burning on my neck…I leaned back against the rock, catching my breath. Above was a rare hole in the clouds, and I could see just a bit of the lavender-and-blue sky up there. Pretty nice view.

"It would be cool if we could stay in this place after dark, wouldn't it?" I said. I imagined being here, sheltered from the wind, waiting for cloud holes like this one to show glimpses of the stars. It always seemed like when the Robot looked up at the stars, he was thinking so much, or maybe *knew* so much, like he had traveled to so many of them. I'd always wished he could tell me about the places he'd been on his amazing ship, where he was actually from....

I dropped my head and sighed, the feeling hitting me all over again. *He's gone, stupid.* "You wouldn't fit into this place anyway," I said, looking back at the sky.

"Fit where?"

"What the—" I jumped at the voice. Suddenly, there was something right beside me! A blur, here in the rocks, but it wasn't some*thing*, it was some*one*.

I was no longer alone in the space. Clare was sitting there with me.

CHAPTER

3

Of course, I didn't know she was Clare yet. I didn't even know *what* she was. All I knew was that there was a girl literally sitting right across from me in the hideout.

"Who are you?" I said breathlessly.

She looked around my age, but unlike me, she wasn't wearing a space suit. Instead, she had on a shimmery black shirt and pants, silvery-looking socks, and no shoes. Her hair was black and wavy and pulled back in a ponytail. She had light brown skin and dark brown eyes.

She glanced around the space like she hadn't heard me.

"Are you from here?" I knew that was a dumb question because that was obviously impossible. And yet, how was she surviving without a suit?

Leaning against the rock, breathing hard, I realized there was something else about her that I couldn't quite wrap my brain around: When she'd appeared, she hadn't just been sitting across from me; there had also been this buzzing feeling in my knees and shins, because in that moment, she'd been occupying the same space as me, like *literally*; our legs had overlapped.

"Hello?" The girl's voice sounded almost distant, like it was on a wind. She looked at the sky, then right past me, then at her own hands.

"Um, hey." My heart was pounding and my whole body felt like an exposed wire.

She blinked hard and held up her hand in front of her, and I could kind of see through it, like she wasn't really a solid object but more like a projection. That made sense with our legs overlapping. She was studying her hand, too, like maybe she was noticing this as well.

I reached out toward the hand she was holding out, and my gloved fingers went right through her.

That made her flinch, and her eyes finally tracked up and seemed to see me.

"You're back," she said.

"I'm—I've been right here."

Her mouth scrunched. "Okay, then *I'm* back. I saw you, but then I was gone for a second. Where am I?" She looked out beyond the tall rocks again.

"Well, you're on a planet, but we don't know exactly where." I took a deep breath and tried to relax. "Who *are* you?" I asked again.

"I'm…" Her face went blank for just a second, like she was in thought. "Sorry, I'm Clare. Clare Williams of the…the salvage ship *Derelict*. That's what I'm supposed to say now, not of…" Her face fell. "Not of Antares B, not anymore."

"Antares?" I said. "You mean like the star?"

Clare looked up at me. As she did, a ripple of light wrinkled across her face. She was definitely some type of hologram or projection or something. "Do you know it?"

"I mean, I know of it. It's a binary star, right? The big one is red."

Clare nodded, but her expression darkened. "Antares A. The destroyer. A red supergiant. We live in its shadow…well, if *shadow* meant its glaring, universe-size brightness."

Okay, so if I was keeping score, this projection of a girl named Clare that had suddenly appeared in front of me was also from another star system. At least I could understand her. A glance at my communicator showed that my translator program was not running.

"We speak the same language," I said.

Clare flicked her head and blinked rapidly. "Not exactly. My real-time translators are running pretty hot. It's weird to hear my voice like this."

I glanced at her hands and wrists, but didn't see any tech there like a communicator or anything. "Your translators?"

Clare peered at me, studying my suit, and nodded to herself. "You...wouldn't know about that, would you? Inter-cortex enhancements. The nanotech install is standard for everyone." She blinked again. "It's like seeing two things at once. Everybody says you get used to it, but..."

"So, are you human?" I asked.

"Human." Clare paused. "Those are the people who migrated from Sol."

"Sol, um, you mean the sun? Migrated?"

"Yeah," said Clare. "Alina says that, judging by your suit technology, facial features, and ancient dialect, you are a human of the twenty-first century. For me, that was many years ago."

"You're from the *future*?"

Clare glanced around again. "I guess so? I mean, it's just regular old present day to me. But you must be one of the original Alpha Centauri colonists."

A wave of nervousness flashed through me. "Um, I guess, except we haven't gotten there yet. I'm part of the twenty-fourth colonist group, but we're lost. It's a long story, but if you're out at Antares in the future then does that mean we're going to make it?"

Clare blinked again, which seemed to indicate that she was reading data. "Alina doesn't have any information on specific colonial groups, or individuals, unfortunately. Maybe if we were still wired to the central cortex, but we lost contact with them."

"Who's Alina?"

"Oh, that's our local intelligence on the *Derelict*. Automated Learning Interactive Network Assistant, I think? One of those words is probably wrong...but don't worry," Clare said, reading the expression on my face. "The Alpha Centauri colonies definitely did succeed. They were the first major post-Earth settlement in the home galactic quadrant. After that—hold on, let me read this...." She squinted like she was trying to focus. "*Homo determinus* expanded out into the second and third galactic quadrants and today occupy settlements in fifty-four star systems."

"*Homo determinus*? Not *sapiens*?"

"*You're Homo sapiens*," said Clare, "but if I remember right from science class, we changed our species name when we began to make upgrades to our bodies using nanotechnology."

"*Determinus*, like you determine your evolution," I guessed. "That's cool. Okay, but if you're from the future, what are you doing here?"

Clare stood up, looked out across the gray ocean, and sighed. "That would be the current life-threatening question. Where to start . . . well, okay, first of all, it turns out that Antares was a stupid place to go live, because it is currently about to go supernova."

"Is that why you called it the destroyer?"

"Yeah. It's so annoying. All my life and my parents' lives and their parents' even, we've known that Antares A was nearing the end of its stellar life cycle, that someday it would go supernova, and that it could happen at any time."

"Then why even go there?" I asked.

Clare shrugged. "Why else? Exo mining, gamma harvesting, gravity assist waypoint, the Antares system has it all.... But I've had to memorize evacuation plans since I was old enough to walk—from our house, from my school, to the nearest spaceport. And now..." She breathed heavily. "It's actually about to happen. We're on our way back to help with the evacuation, but something's gone wrong."

"On your way back...so you're on a ship right now? I mean, the rest of you?"

Clare nodded. "The *Derelict*. My family's ship."

As she said this, another ripple flashed across her, and for a second she disappeared completely. I found myself just looking at the rocks, hearing only the sound of the wind and waves—

Then she was back. She shook her head, dazed. "Did I—sorry. That was weird." She rubbed her head. "I was just back on my ship for a minute."

"You disappeared," I said.

"It was like I blinked, and I was there. And everyone was shouting, all the emergency systems freaking out. We're in so much trouble, and I'm… what am I doing here?"

I could barely keep up with what Clare was saying, so I tried to focus on one question at a time. "What happened to your ship?"

"That's the thing. I don't really know; I don't think my parents quite know yet, either, at least not based on how they keep shouting. We were far out on a salvage mission near the BiFlexion Reach—sorry, that's the very outer edge of the nebula that Antares A creates. It's really beautiful, if you don't mind deadly radiation. We were on our way to salvage a junker that had been abandoned and presumed lost; my parents had gotten a tip about its location. The price for junked ships has been going up since Antares started making more rumblings like it might collapse. I guess when you're going to evacuate a planet, any ship is a good ship.

"Anyway, we'd almost reached it when the call came from home: Helium levels in the core of

Antares A had dropped past the critical threshold. The supernova will happen any time now. So, we turned and burned for home. Our ship has been commissioned to carry two hundred evacuees. But on the way we've run into something.... I think my brother might be hurt." She closed her eyes tightly for a moment. "I can't tell. I can't see it now."

"You have a brother?" I asked.

"Yeah," said Clare, rolling her eyes. "He's so annoying—sorry, are you somebody's brother?"

"Yeah, I have two sisters."

"Well, you're probably a good one. You've already listened to me for ten times longer than my brother ever would."

I couldn't help smiling. "I think I know the feeling. So, you say you ran into something?"

"Yeah. We were flying along, and suddenly all the ship's systems started going haywire, things shorting out and shaking and my parents running around. I heard Dad shouting a bunch of garble from the engine room about temporal phasing in the engine's vacuum core. He asked me to bring him some tools and I literally just went in there with him, like a minute ago—and then the lights started flashing and—*zip!* Here I was, sitting in this little spot across from a kid in an orange suit." She looked around. "On some dreary planet."

"Wow," I said. This was unbelievable. "But you're not really here. I mean, you're like a projection. But your...mind is here? Is that right?"

"Maybe that's more accurate. All my senses and data are telling me I'm here, except..." She waved her hand, and her fingers flashed right through the rock. "Pretty weird, huh?"

"Yeah." I thought of the portal in the cave on our last planet, of stepping through and traveling back to Earth, of briefly being on that massive alien ship. "But weird things can happen in space. So, when you just blinked away a second ago, was, like, *all* of you back on your ship? Had any time passed there?"

Clare thought for a moment. "Yeah, I was lying

on the floor, on my back, like maybe I'd fallen down? And I felt whole there, not like here."

"Does Alina know what's happened to you, or your ship?" I asked.

"Not yet. So far she's referring to whatever we ran into as a *space-time anomaly.*"

"It sounds like that's what transported you here."

"Right." Clare looked over her shoulder, even though there was nothing there. "I need to get back. If we're in trouble, I…" She closed her eyes tight, and I heard her saying quietly, "Wake up, wake up."

"I don't think this is a dream," I said. "I mean, *I'm* not a dream."

Clare opened her eyes and sighed. "I know. I wasn't hoping that you were. I mean, except that I was. But how can I be here, wherever this is? There are no planets like this in our star system."

"Ours, either." I thought of the Robot's engine, the one that had brought us here and was now lying dormant in our cargo hold, the same kind that powered the *Resolute.* "There are ways that you can get across the galaxy fast…." That reminded me of the doorway in the cave again. "You didn't run into any guys in black cloaks with red goggle eyes, did you?"

Clare's brow wrinkled. "No. At least not that I saw."

"They *are* invisible sometimes…."

"What are you talking about?"

"Sorry, nothing, just thinking of ways you might have ended up here."

"Hang on." Clare winced. "Aah…" A ripple passed through her and she sort of blipped out for a second. Then she was back. There were tears in her eyes. "That hurt."

"Did you see anything that time?"

"The engine room. I had just enough time to sit up and look around before I flashed back here. And…I felt a lot of pain. It's like I'm being torn apart."

"I'm sorry," I said. "That sucks."

"Pretty much. But I did hear Alina refer to the

thing we ran into as a *quantum field rift*. Does that mean anything to you?"

"No. Sorry."

Clare suddenly smiled. "I haven't even asked you your name."

"Oh man, I'm sorry; I'm Will Robinson, of the, um, the *Jupiter 2*."

"Is that your ship?"

"Yeah. We're out of fuel and stranded here."

"Did you come here through some kind of rift, too?"

"Sort of, but not like the one you're talking about."

"And you have no idea where 'here' is."

A memory flashed through my mind, of first arriving in this system, and of what the Robot had said about this place: *Danger*.

"No," I said.

Clare looked at the triangle rock formation around us. "This is kind of a cool little spot."

"Yeah. I just found it."

Clare stood and peered through the gaps. "Your ship's that way, I take it?"

"How'd you know?" I said, following her gaze. The *Jupiter* was hidden behind the Serpent's head.

"Well, I don't see a boat, and there's no land in any other direction. Ooh…" She looked at the waves. "It doesn't look like there's going to be any land in *your* direction for much longer, either."

She was right; the long spit of sand between me and the Serpent head had started to shrink. The largest waves were already lapping over and briefly meeting in the center. "Yeah, I should probably—"

I turned and Clare was gone. There were no marks in the sand. Like she'd never been there.

Except then, *zap!* She was back, her mouth moving, only this time there was no sound coming out.

"Clare? Hey." I waved my arms at her. "I'm right here."

There were tears now in her wide eyes. She looked around like she was blind, and then her gaze suddenly snapped to me. Another ripple of electricity passed through her holographic body—

"Will!" she said, her voice edged with static. "It's getting worse here, I—"

Disappeared.

Just wind.

Then back again. "We're trying to move away from the rift, but we're in trouble!"

"Is there anything I can do?" I said helplessly.

"I don't know, I—I'm trying to—"

A flash and she was gone again.

Now back. "This is getting hard to handle. I feel like I'm going to pass out."

"I want to help," I said. "I just don't know how."

Clare looked out beyond the rocks. "You need to go," she said.

"You don't need to worry about me." Except, checking the tide, I realized she was definitely right.

"Can you come back later?" Clare asked.

"Um, yeah, I mean, there will be another low tide tonight, although I'm not sure it will be low enough to make it back to this spot—plus it would be tough in the dark and wind." *Not to mention that Mom and Dad would never let me,* I thought. "But I can definitely get out here again tomorrow morning. Can *you* still come back here?"

Clare was breathing hard, her face red. "Just tell me how long it will be until you can get back to this spot, and I'll figure it out."

"But how would you even do that—"

"Will, please!" A double ripple of jagged static passed through her. "Just tell me and I'll try. And if we never see each other again, it was nice to meet you."

I swiped through screens on my communicator until I found the tide table I'd made with Mom. "I can be back in nineteen hours"—that number might sound odd, but the days are shorter on this planet than on Earth—"will that work?" I didn't add: *Will your ship even survive that long?*

Clare managed to smile. "Let's try, okay?"

"Okay," I said, nodding to her.

"Great. Well, until—"

She winked away.

I waited, counting to myself. *One...two...three... four...*

But I got all the way to thirty and she hadn't returned.

I stood there for another minute, the wind elbowing me, the sound of slapping waves growing louder. What the heck had just happened? Looking around, I could almost convince myself that it had all been a dream.

But no, that had been real, I was sure of it. I mean, considering everything we had seen since we'd left Earth, I could reasonably say that meeting some sort of transmission of a girl from the future was more likely than me losing my mind, or at least *as* likely.

Speaking of likely, I glanced back and saw that, *uh-oh*, the waves were about to cover my route.

I stepped out of the sunken spot beneath the three triangle rocks. "I'll be back," I said to the hideout, to Clare, wherever she was. And then I turned and jogged across the long, straight, rapidly disappearing sandbar as fast as I dared, knowing I couldn't afford a wrong step. By the time I got back to the rock that was across the channel from the Serpent's head, the waves were lapping at my ankles. Could I make the jump back across?

It turned out that I could.

It turned out I could get all the way back home safely.

And later, it turned out all of that had been the least of my worries.

CHAPTER

4

"This is Will Robinson of the twenty-fourth colonist group, and I have made a major discovery... I think."

I was back on our island. Everyone except Mom was on board the *Jupiter*—I knew I'd get no privacy in there—so I was sitting on the sand underneath the ship, leaning against one of the landing struts, the one farthest from the greenhouse and the air lock. I had my video recorder out and had ported it into my communicator so it could pick up my voice without me having to use the speaker on my helmet.

I'd said *I think* because you know that feeling

when something is so strange or different than the rest of your life that you have to remind yourself it actually happened? That was what meeting Clare felt like.

And I had no evidence, except for that little shell in my pocket.

"I have made contact with a future human," I continued for my recording, "who was somehow projected across space to this location." I kicked myself for not even trying to take a picture of Clare, although that would have been sort of rude. *Hey, girl-from-the-future-who's-in-a-star-exploding-crisis, smile!* But I should have at least run a scan of her or something, even if I'd had to do it secretly.

Maybe I'd get another chance. I couldn't stop thinking about how I was going to get the earliest start possible the next morning to get back out there.

"Actually, she's not exactly a human. They call themselves—" I paused my recording because my neck had flared up again, and it felt like it was on fire, the worst it had been. I scratched uselessly at my suit and realized I was kind of breathing hard, too, even though I was just sitting here. I closed my eyes and it settled down, enough that I could get back to my video.

I recounted everything that Clare had told me about her situation. "I should have more to report when I go back tomorrow," I finished. "Hopefully, she'll be there." As I stopped the recording, I felt a little nervous rush. I really did hope Clare would show up again. We had so much more to figure out! There was everything that was happening to her, but then there was also the fact that people from the future might have some ideas about how we could un-strand ourselves from this planet.... But also, it had just been nice to be talking to someone my own age, no matter if she was a projection or not. A fellow young space traveler like me.

At the same time, I knew the first thing I needed to do was tell Mom and Dad, and while I was excited to share my discovery, the thought also caused a nervous wave inside me. Sometimes their reaction to unknown or dangerous stuff was to *keep* me from it, like how they'd been so apprehensive about the Robot. In fact, sometimes I even felt like if it wasn't for them, things might have gone differently, and the Robot wouldn't be gone. And I did not want that to happen with Clare.

I put away my recorder and headed inside. Pulling off my helmet and inhaling the sweet, damp greenhouse air only made the last hour seem even more surreal. My fingers flew to the back of my neck and started scratching furiously. The skin felt bumpy, a little oily, and really hot.

I hung up my helmet and put my breathing pack on its charger. I took the shell I'd found over to the sample sterilizer, a rectangular metal box with a door on the front, sort of like an oven. I placed the shell inside and activated the system. The machine hummed and flashed with ultraviolet light. After a minute, a green light blinked and it shut off, and I removed the shell.

I looked down at my suit, realizing that it was damp and laced with sand. Since I'd been to new and "uncharted" spots, Mom would want me to run it through the ionizing dryer, which would dry it out thoroughly and also sterilize it, but I really wasn't in the mood to traipse through the ship in just my thermals, which I'd also started outgrowing—Dad had even called the pants "high waters," which was an old Earth expression—so I decided to change first and then run my suit.

"I'll be right back," I said to the clear door of the dryer, over on the far side of the garage.

I headed up the ladder to the main hall. On my way to my compartment, I overheard Dad and Don conferring about something in the direction of the engine room.

"How am I supposed to know?" I heard Dad saying. "Maureen is the expert on that."

"Yeah," Don was saying, "but I've been expressly forbidden from bringing my unique brand of humor to her office door uninvited. Could you ask her?"

"I'll see what she thinks," Dad said.

I stopped by my compartment and exchanged my suit for sweats. I added the new shell to my collection, which was in a neat row across my clothing locker. I looked at my model of the Robot and smiled. "You would have liked her," I said, thinking of Clare again. *The Robot might have been able to help her, too.* Once again, I felt full of frustration and loneliness.

I brought my suit back to the ionizer and headed for the hub to get lunch. Penny and Judy were both there, Penny still curled with her notebook on her knees, exactly as I'd left her hours before, her pen scribbling along. Judy was at the round table in the center of the room, flipping through a medical textbook on her reader. She'd been keeping herself busy by retaking her med school courses, even the exams. No surprise, she was getting straight As again. The page she was looking at now had a diagram of some kind of joint.

"Hey," Penny said to me without looking up.

This got Judy's attention. "Will, you're back."

"Of course he's back. He's standing right there," Penny muttered.

Sometimes you could tell we'd been cooped up together for six months.

Judy frowned at her. "How was your nature walk?" she asked me.

"It wasn't a nature walk," I said, immediately feeling a flash of annoyance.

"He's an intrepid explorer," Penny said, writing away.

"Shut up," I said.

"What? I was serious!" said Penny. "You're out there charting the unknown reaches of"—her face started to crack into a laugh—"the great continent of Moist Sandia."

"Whatever." I started out.

"Hold on." I heard Judy's chair move and realized that I'd been scratching my neck as I turned.

"Why?" I took another step—

Judy caught my shoulder. "Hey, doctor's orders."

"Can't believe you gave her a chance to say that," Penny piped up.

Judy ignored her and touched my neck. "Has this been feeling worse?" she asked.

"I don't know. It has been pretty itchy a couple of times.... Does it look worse?"

"Maybe." Suddenly, she was going full Judy, pulling a latex glove from her pocket and snapping it on. She held up her communicator and took a photo. "Look."

She moved her wrist so I could see. Okay, *ew.* The red area looked kind of bubbly, and there were these white dots here and there. "Are they oozing?" I asked.

"They are, indeed."

"Ooh, wait!" Penny dropped her notebook and jumped up. "Remember: If it oozes or has weird grossness, I demand to see."

Judy huffed. "These almost look like stings. Remember the yellow jackets when we were little?"

"You mean those bees?" said Penny.

"They weren't bees," said Judy. "There haven't been bees in the wild since our parents were kids."

I felt Judy's breath on my neck. And now a pinching sensation that made me flinch.

"What are you doing?"

"Stay still. I'm looking for stingers."

"I didn't get stung by a stupid yellow jacket on

this planet!" I said. "It's the same allergy I've had for days now."

"Maybe," said Judy, "but that doesn't mean that whatever is causing this hasn't…" She trailed off.

Worry flashed through me. "Hasn't what?"

"I don't know," said Judy. "Hold on." I winced as Judy squeezed an area of my neck skin between her fingers. I felt a light scratch and glanced back to see that she had run a little swab over my neck. It came away with yellowish streaks.

"Oh yeah," said Penny, grinning but also stepping away from me. "That's the good stuff."

"What is it?" I asked.

Judy peered at the yellow streaks. "Pus, most likely. That's usually less a sign of an allergic reaction and more of an infection. I'll analyze it." She produced a little sample bag from the pouch on her belt and put the swab in. "You're sure you haven't torn your suit or anything when you've been out exploring?"

"I would have known if I'd torn my suit."

"And you haven't snared your oxygen tank on anything?"

"No, why?"

"I'm just trying to figure out how you were exposed to something that none of the rest of us seem to have been exposed to, so I'm thinking about how things spread. Has there been *anything* out of the ordinary on your walks?"

"Um, this whole place is out of the ordinary," said Penny.

Judy frowned at her. "I'm serious, Will. Anything at all?"

"Maybe...," I said, my heart skipping a beat.

"Will." Judy turned me around by my shoulders. "Explain. What did you find?"

"Ooh, did we make a discovery?" Mom walked in, her attention half on a tablet she was tapping.

Don't tell them! I thought immediately. "Nothing, really." Except of course I needed to tell them. And I wanted to...didn't I? Clare's appearance was a massive discovery that changed everything we thought we knew about our universe, about our own future! Not to mention how her future tech might be helpful. Also, it had crossed my mind that the space-time rift Clare had run into might also be dangerous to us.

"He's definitely hiding something," said Penny, glancing at Judy.

"Spill it," said Judy.

"Yeah, Will. What's the big secret?" said Mom, her eyes darting from the tablet to me.

"There are secrets?" Now Dad entered, too!

"Will's keeping something from us," Penny said immediately.

"I'm not—shut up!" I threw up my hands. "Would you give me a chance to talk?"

They all closed their mouths, barely hiding grins.

"Okay, so, I found a new spot farther from here, and I sort of had an encounter."

"An *encounter*?" said Mom, her face getting serious.

"What's that supposed to mean?" Penny asked.

"I kinda met someone," I said nervously. "I mean, not really someone, but, yeah. It was a girl from another spaceship."

"Another *Jupiter*?" Judy nearly jumped.

"Where are they?" said Dad.

"No, not a *Jupiter*, not even close! Just listen: She's actually from another star system, I mean, she's from the future, technically...."

"Was she human?" Penny asked, her face suddenly pale. "Or more like a black-cloaked goggle-wearing time traveler?"

"Huh?" said Dad, looking at her quizzically.

"What are you talking about?" Judy asked, with a similar look.

"Nothing," Penny said quickly. She'd been referring to the beings we had run into on our last planet, through the time portal in the cave when Penny had stolen the candy. But because of how the Robot had fixed things afterward, only Penny and I remembered any of that.

"This was a girl," I continued, "like my age. She's human, except she's from the future. But she wasn't all here. She was more like a projection, caused by some sort of space-time rift. A quantum disturbance."

I caught Mom and Dad exchanging a look.

"Okay…," Judy said. "Did this space-time-projection-rift-girl-person have a name?"

"Clare."

"Clare." Judy reached for my forehead. "Do you feel feverish?"

"No."

"What about your pulse?" She took my wrist. "I should have checked that."

"Stop, my pulse is fine. But—"

"You're saying this happened out at the rocks," said Mom, "while you were exploring." She'd crossed her arms. "Were you feeling feverish out there?"

"No—I mean, yeah, a little, but that doesn't matter. I didn't hallucinate her."

"Will," Judy said, and her tone got soft, like a gentle doctor's voice about to tell me my condition was terminal. She sounded exactly like Mom. "I think we understand what *Clare* is."

"What's that supposed to mean?"

"It means it's okay, we get it," said Penny.

"Get what?"

Judy made a very Mom-like face, the one when

she was about to try to "break it to you." "It's perfectly natural for you to invent an imaginary friend considering that you lost—"

"What? She's not imaginary!" I shouted. "Why would you say that?"

"Okay, I'm sorry," said Judy, raising her hands.

Penny looked away. "It just kind of sounds like an imaginary friend is all—"

"Whatever, fine!" I turned toward the doorway.

"Hold on, Will," said Dad. He eyed Penny and Judy. "Guys, settle down."

"Will," said Mom, "I think the girls were just trying to empathize, not diminish whatever you saw out there."

"We all know you've been going through some hard feelings lately," Dad added.

"This isn't about the Robot!" I shouted. "If you guys aren't going to listen—I didn't even want to tell you, anyway."

"No, it's always good to tell us," said Dad.

"We want to know," said Mom. "And if you

encountered something out of the ordinary on this planet, we *need* to know. I just think what you're describing sounds pretty…" Her mouth scrunched.

"What?" I asked.

"Unlikely, that's all. Not impossible, but…"

"You know what? You're right," I said suddenly. "It does sound ridiculous." I rubbed my head. "I think I just need to lie down for a minute."

"And put on another antihistamine patch," said Judy.

"Right, and that."

"Okay," said Dad, sounding confused. "But this thing you saw…"

I could tell now that I needed to show them some kind of proof about Clare. Otherwise they weren't going to believe me, and if I kept pushing it, they might not even let me go back out there tomorrow. "I don't even know if I saw anything," I said. "You guys might be right. I've been feeling a lot lately. And this rash is making me irrational. And we're lost on this planet."

Mom stepped over and hugged me. "It's okay, honey. It's a hard time."

"For sure," Penny echoed.

"Yeah, thanks," I said. I pulled away from Mom. "I'll be in my compartment."

"I'll check on you in a little bit," said Mom.

"Okay." I turned, leaving them all there, and walked down the corridor to my compartment, where I shut the door and threw myself down on my bunk. "Imaginary friend," I muttered to myself. That sounded like such little-kid stuff!

I lay there staring at the ceiling, my fists balled in frustration, and then my eyes returned to my Robot model. "You would have believed me," I said. "You wouldn't have needed any evidence." But then I realized that I was basically doing the same thing they'd just accused me of—talking to someone who wasn't there—and I punched my mattress.

I got a new antihistamine patch out of my med kit, put it on my wrist, and closed my eyes. I took deep breaths and tried to picture our old planet, the Robot and me tromping through the woods, climbing the rocks, playing tic-tac-toe. *I wish you were here right now.*

The itching started to subside. As I calmed down, I thought about Clare. What kind of thing could she and her family have run into that would make her appear across the galaxy? It had to be some sort of wormhole, didn't it? Sort of like the portal technology that the beings on our last planet had. It still seemed possible that maybe they had something to do with this—

My thoughts got cut off when the ship's emergency lights, the only ones we regularly used, blinked off, then back on. And then all the lights in my room flashed on, including the overhead ones that we hadn't used since we'd arrived. I squinted, throwing a hand over my eyes. *Those lights shouldn't be coming on—*

And now an alarm sounded.

"Warning!" the *Jupiter*'s emergency computer announced. "Life support levels critical! Prepare for immediate evacuation!"

CHAPTER

5

I bolted up. What was happening? It had to be another corrosion leak—had I missed a spot?—but I checked my communicator and it wasn't giving any dangerous atmospheric readings.

"Suits on!" I heard Judy shout, followed by the pounding of her boots as she ran by. "Suits on!"

Oh no, my suit was still in the ionizer! I jumped out of bed and ran down the hall. The air already felt thin in my chest. I half climbed, half slid down the ladder and ran for the machine, past where Penny and Judy were clipping their helmets in place. Dr. Smith stood beside them, already in her suit, her hands handcuffed in front of her.

"I'm surprised you're bothering to give me a suit, considering the way you've been treating me," said Smith dryly. "Oh, hello, Will. You're awfully underdressed—"

"Oh quiet!" shouted Penny, shoving Smith's helmet into her hands.

"Warning! Life support levels critical!" The message repeated.

"What's going on?" I shouted over the noise.

Judy just shook her head. "We have no idea."

I stopped the ionizer, yanked out my suit, and started tugging it over my feet. "My communicator isn't picking up anything!"

"Neither is mine, but we can't risk it," said Judy. "Make sure you've got your suits in power-saving mode! If life support really is out, then—"

Suddenly, the warning tone stopped.

"Disregard alert," the computer announced. "Life support levels normal."

"Will!" It was Dad, calling over the ship-wide comms.

"Dad, what's going on?"

"Get down here!"

"Do I need my suit?"

"No, we're inside. Under the cockpit."

"Ooh, can I go?" said Smith.

"You are going straight back to your cell," said Penny, leading Smith by the cuffs.

"Must be nice to be so important," Smith muttered to me as Penny dragged her past.

I didn't answer. Ever since on our last planet when Smith had tricked me into helping her escape, my goal was to interact with her as little as possible.

I returned my suit to the ionizer and climbed back up to the hall, where I found one of the floor hatches open just outside the cockpit doorway. I knelt and peered inside. Dad and Don were crouched in a narrow sub-compartment surrounded by big bundles of wiring. They were both wearing headlamps and had opened a circuit panel in the wall.

"What happened?" I asked.

"Good question," said Don.

"Power surge," said Dad. "A nasty one."

"Things are cycling back up to normal now," said Don. "But yeah, that wasn't pretty. Drained the batteries thirty percent in under a minute. We're going to have to ration for a few days just to get back to safe levels."

"A surge from what?" I asked. "The solar panels?"

Don shook his head. "They don't make enough power in a week to turn all the lights on in this ship."

The emergency lights blinked overhead, and there was a low hum in the floor. "Okay, I think we're good," said Dad. He and Don unclipped their helmets, and I climbed down into the compartment beside them.

Don slid one of the large circuit boards down from the wall and peered at it, running his head-lamp slowly back and forth over the geometric pattern. "Look at the scoring on these transistors." He rubbed his finger over one of the little knob-like structures, and it came away with a filmy, black resin. "It's like they all nearly overheated at once, completely evenly, which is impossible, unless…"

"Unless what?" said Dad.

Don ran a hand through his hair and blew air out of his cheeks. "Well, unless there was an energy source in the air, something that could hit all the transistors at once without having to run through the circuit pathways, thus bypassing the breakers."

"Like that lightning we keep seeing on the horizon?" I wondered aloud.

"Maybe," said Don. He tapped his communicator. "Sensors did record a two-millisecond electromagnetic spike right before this."

"So that's it?" said Dad.

"Not exactly. Lightning usually coalesces into a bolt, and if the *Jupiter* had actually been struck by lightning, this would look very different."

"Plus, the ship would have acted as a Faraday cage," I said, crouching beside them.

"Care to keep me up to speed on whatever you're talking about?" said Dad.

"He's right," said Don. "The *Jupiter's* body would've transferred most of the lightning energy straight into the ground. Some systems would've definitely been fried, but it certainly wouldn't look like this."

"Okay, so it's not the lightning. Then what is it?"

I peered at the circuit panel Don was holding. Mom often had me do spot checks on the panels around the ship, and I could see what Don was talking about: the charred color on the end of each transistor.

"Could it be some kind of energy field?" I asked.

"That is what it looks like," said Don, "but that kind of thing should only really happen in a vacuum environment, not here in the atmosphere."

"Why did you ask that?" said Dad, eyeing me.

"Just...trying to think it through." I didn't feel like getting into it again and dealing with all the disbelief and skepticism about Clare, about *me*, but it had crossed my mind that maybe the rift that had made Clare appear was affecting us, too. I could try to find out more from her tomorrow, and then, if this really *was* related, I'd have something concrete to say that wouldn't have everyone treating me like a little kid.

"Whatever it was, things seem all right now," said Don. "But if it happens again…it could get a lot worse."

"Define *worse*," said Dad.

Don shrugged. "Something like a cascading systems failure that could kill us all. Hold on."

"What now?" Dad asked.

Don held the board aside and peered into the slot. He ran his finger along the base of the frame, then held it up. It was glistening with a spot of greenish fluid.

"What is that, engine fluid?" said Dad. It did have a sort of oily look to it.

Don smelled it, and his nose wrinkled. "Sour. It looks more like something organic."

Dad groaned. "Our last planet had eels in the fuel lines. Please don't tell me this one has something else that wants to eat our ship."

"Unlikely, but you'd better scan it just to be sure." Don pulled off his glove and handed it to

Dad. "Will and I can check these other boards to see how widespread this is."

Dad took the glove and frowned at it. "I'll have Judy run it. Here, you're more use down here than I am." He handed me his headlamp and climbed out.

Don pulled out the next board and placed it on the floor, then removed another.

I peered at the circuit pathways and saw the same black char.

"If this burst had lasted even a few seconds longer, these entire systems could have been completely fried," said Don.

"There's scoring on the insulation," I noted, "like it partially melted."

"Okay, so we need to protect these things somehow," Don said, "but we don't exactly have the supplies or the hundreds of hours it would take to add shielding to every system on the ship."

"What if we reversed the charge?" I said. "If this electrical field returns, we need the circuits to not absorb that energy. Like charges repel, right?"

Don's eyes lit up. "You're talking about switching

the polarity on the systems." He nodded. "The only problem would be that the systems wouldn't work."

"What if it was only for a millisecond or two? Like, only in response to the electromagnetic spike you recorded? That might counter the field before it could fry everything," I said.

"It could work…." Don looked at the rack of circuit boards. "If I set up a battery with reverse polarity on the backup circuit channel—at the panel coupling, not on each board—I suppose we could then program the *Jupiter* to flip the switch the moment a spike is detected." Don patted my shoulder. "That, my friend, is genius. See, I knew there was a reason we kept you around."

I smiled and felt my face getting red. "Thanks."

"Now, since you're still young enough for me to give you orders, head up to my compartment and grab my green supply bag. That's where I keep the spare cells."

"Got it." I went for the bag, and Don and I spent the rest of the afternoon wiring up the panels. The work had to be precise, and for long stretches of time I managed to forget about the itching on my neck, and there were even a couple of moments when I forgot about Clare. But once I got the wiring routines down, my thoughts drifted to the next day and meeting up with her again.

ONE DAY BEFORE
LOWEST TIDE

CHAPTER

6

"Rise and shine, Farmer W—"

"Yeah, I'm up." I met Dad in the doorway, already dressed and zipping up my pack.

"Oh, hey." He smiled. "Somebody's anxious to check those potassium levels."

"Let's get to it." I didn't bother mentioning that I'd already been up for an hour with the anticipation for the day, not to mention the itching on my neck.

Dad noticed my bag. "You have somewhere to be?"

"Today's the second lowest tide of the cycle," I said. "I want to do some more exploring."

"All right, well, don't skimp on your chores."

We headed down to the garden and I quickly did my probes.

"Everything look okay?" said Dad as I walked over to him.

"Yup, we're good." I knew he wanted the detailed report, but I fought the urge to give it to him, instead checking my communicator to make sure I was still on time.

"Well, take a look at this." Dad held out his hand, revealing a few cherry tomatoes. "Best ratio of size to skin integrity we've had yet." He plucked one between his fingers and popped it in his mouth.

I knew I was supposed to take one, too—tasting our successes was another part of our morning routine—but instead I said, "Cool," and started pulling on my helmet. "I already had an energy bar."

"Oh. Okay." Dad's face fell. He ate another one before lining up the rest on the control table. "You're missing out," he said.

We stepped out into the morning wind, the suns not yet up, and as we ducked beneath the *Jupiter*, I paused. The terrain looked different.

"Lot of wave action last night with the big high tide," said Dad, moving toward the first landing strut.

That made sense. With the extreme low tides came extreme highs as well, but I was still surprised to see how much had changed. There was a hollowed-out area to one side of the ship, exposing a set of rocks that we'd never seen before, and a mounded formation on another. There was also a wide eroded area over by the rocks beside Mom's office, creating a little bay of water. The sight of all these changes made me worry. What would this have done to the spot where I was meeting Clare? Would I even still be able to reach it?

I made my checks of the hull and went over to Dad while he was still inspecting the last landing strut. "All fine," I reported. "I'm going to go. See you later."

"Okay. Have fun. After this, I'll be helping Don install more of those battery work-arounds you two came up with. It would go a lot faster if you could help when you get back."

"I'll come find you."

"Sounds good."

I wondered if he'd ask me anything else about where I was going, if he even remembered what I'd been saying the day before, but he just peered back into the machinery.

I still felt a twinge of guilt as I left. I'd spent so many years wishing Dad had been around more, looking out at audiences and sidelines and wishing I'd see him there, and now here I was, taking off when I knew he wanted to spend time with me. And yet, as I hurried across the sand, a surge of relief coursed through me. I was on time to reach the rocks before the tide was at its absolute lowest.

I stopped just as I was passing the bluff. Even though I wanted to head straight to the new spot, I turned and ducked into Mom's office.

"Who dares disturb the mad scientist at work?" she called from over her shoulder.

That made me smile. "Hey."

Mom turned from her table and blinked hard, like her eyes were already tired from studying her charts. "Oh, Will. You're up and at 'em early."

"Not as early as you," I said.

Mom shook her head. "No rest for the obsessed."

I nodded. "Yeah."

"Headed out exploring?"

"Uh-huh, I just—"

"Want some company?"

That stopped me in my tracks. "Oh. I mean, aren't you busy?"

Mom spread her hands over her table. "Yes, but it occurs to me that I am *always* busy, so why not play hooky for an hour?"

"Um…"

"I realize we were kind of harsh yesterday in the hub. It might be cool to see what you've been discovering—unless this isn't a good time."

I had looked away, and now I couldn't quite meet her eyes. Yesterday I had wanted them to know about Clare, but after how they'd reacted...now I just wanted to get the proof on my own. "It's actually, um...it's not the best time right now? I mean, that would be fun, just, this morning I had some stuff I wanted to do on my own."

"But..." Mom was looking at me with her concerned expression. "Aren't you always on your own?"

"I guess." The Robot's glowing face flashed in my mind. I hadn't *always* been. "It's fine, Mom. You don't need to worry."

"I'm not worried." Mom looked at me for another second, like she was studying me.

Yeah, right, I thought.

Then she turned back to her work. "You have fun."

"Thanks." I turned to go but then paused. I was so anxious to get out of there that I nearly forgot the reason I'd stopped by in the first place. "Hey, can I borrow the RF scanner? Unless you're using it."

"Oh, um, sure." Mom reached across her table for the small black instrument, but before she handed it to me, she checked her charts. "The next lightning storm isn't for a week...so I have to ask, my scientist son, what do you need it for? Does this have something to do with what Don was going on about yesterday? Some sort of energy burst? He said you guys fixed it."

"Yeah, we did, but I just thought I'd gather readings on my hike. I don't think I'll pick up anything, but it can't hurt, right? A good scientist is a thorough scientist?"

Mom smiled. "So said a famous scientist and mother." She handed me the scanner. "Careful with that. Nearest tech support is an unknown number of light-years away."

"Thanks."

I stowed the scanner in my pack on my way out.

"Will," Mom called. "I do want to come along. Maybe next time?"

"Sure." She smiled at me, and I returned it as best I could, then hurried out.

Finally, I was on my way, around the bluff, over the Whaleback, across the Pools and along the

Serpent, whose twisting back had changed shape slightly in the waves overnight. It had lost a section, too, but the gap was one I could jump over. As I climbed the Serpent's head, my pulse quickened. It wasn't going to be there, I just knew it wasn't—

But yes! Ahead, I saw the long spine of sand and, far in the distance, the triangle rocks. In fact, not only were they there, but the rocks looked a little taller, as if the sand around them had eroded further.

The rock below me, however, the one I had to jump across the deep channel to reach, was still only just peeking out of the water, so I sat on the edge of the Serpent's head and waited for the tide to fall a little farther. While I waited, I got out the RF scanner and waved it around. No evidence of energy pulses, like lightning would make. I also used my communicator's scanning tool to check for microwaves and gamma rays, neither of which should have been possible, and sure enough, both readings came out negative.

After twenty minutes, the tide had lowered enough to expose the far rock. I leaped across and jogged down the long sandbar that led to the triangle rocks. As I got closer, I thought I saw movement there. Would she really be back? I checked my watch; it had been eighteen and a half hours....

But when I got to the triangle formation, Clare wasn't there. The rocks definitely seemed taller, and peering into the space between them, I saw that the sand floor was lower than the day before, too, as if it had been hollowed out by the waves.

But what really caught my attention were the three gnarled pieces of what looked like driftwood logs crisscrossing the top of the triangle. The logs were dark gray and metallic looking, and there were pieces of the bioluminescent kelp draped over them, creating a sort of glowy ceiling to the space between the rocks. There were also pieces of the kelp hanging on the inside faces of two of the rocks, about halfway up. They hung from pointy shells that looked like larger versions of the one I had found the day before. I stood there staring at the structure, my fingers rubbing my suit above my neck, which had started to itch again. The way everything was arranged seemed like it couldn't have just been random, from the wind or the waves. It looked almost...decorated?

"Do you like it?"

Clare appeared on the far side of the rocks. She was wearing a futuristic-looking space suit and was carrying another piece of driftwood that was nearly as tall as her. Her suit was slick and purplish black, with a helmet that was more rectangular than ours, and clear on all four sides.

"You're back," I said, grinning.

"I told you I'd be here." She dropped the piece of driftwood into the space between the rocks, and when it hit the side of the rock, it made a clanging sound. "This stuff is heavy," she said, breathing hard.

If she was carrying something, and if she needed to be wearing a suit, that meant: "You're like, *here* here now, aren't you? Like, solid."

"Oh, yeah." Clare motioned to her suit. "Turns out this planet you're on is super poisonous, huh?"

She held out her hand. "Now we can meet like proper explorers."

I reached out and grasped her gloved hand in mine, and we shook, like two totally solid and *not* imaginary beings.

"So, what do you think?" She motioned to the driftwood and the moss. "I thought our fort could use some spiffying up."

Our fort. That made me smile. "I like it. Where did you find this?" I said, running my hand over the smooth driftwood. "We haven't seen anything like it."

"There are new tide pools over here. Come on, I'll show you." She stepped around to the opposite side of the rocks, where up until that morning there had been only water. I followed and saw that there was a new area of sandbar that was just peeking out from the waves, dotted with tide pools surrounded by low black rocks.

"Hold on," I said. "How are you here? Like, all the way? What's been happening on your ship? Do you have time to be, you know, decorating?"

"Oh." Clare paused and a shadow crossed her face. "I was trying not to think about that....It's not good. The rift—that's what my parents are officially calling it—totally overloaded our ship's systems. We're dead in the water. Everyone's asleep now, or at least, trying to get some sleep. So, I just came back here."

"An overload?" I said. "Was it like a power surge?"

"I think so. Why?"

"Something like that happened on our ship, too. But not as serious."

"Well, I hope the *exact* same thing doesn't happen to you," Clare said, bending down at the nearest of the new tide pools. "Nearly all our systems are offline." She pointed to a little piece of kelp rolling back and forth at the edge of the pool. "We're basically like that, and the more we drift, the closer we get to the edge of the rift. Which is maybe why my presence here is stronger? But I don't know what's going to happen if the ship hits it."

"How much time do you have?" I asked, kneeling beside her.

"If we can't get the ship back online, then we only have as long as our suit batteries can last, so... a couple of days? We've been sending distress signals, but since everyone on our planet is focused on evacuating before the supernova, there's not exactly time to worry about our little family."

"And how'd you get back here, like, all the way?"

"Remember how I was telling you that the rift seemed to be strongest in our engine room? After the power surge, Dad said it was off-limits, but I snuck back down when everyone was asleep. There's this weird light glowing all around the engine's vacuum core, and when I got near it, it sort of washed over me and—*zip!*—I was here, just like the first time, only solid, like the effect of the rift has gotten stronger. I guess because we're closer to it. I wasn't ready for that, so when I showed up here, I started gasping and choking and had to jump back through the rift before I suffocated. But then I came back prepared." She motioned to her suit.

"Jump back through," I said, looking around and seeing no sign of any kind of rift nearby. "How?"

"I can see it." Clare looked over her shoulder. "The rift is right there, behind me, but not really here. It's almost like it's in the back of my head.... It's hard to describe."

"Okay, wow. Can any of your family members travel like this?"

Clare shrugged. "They haven't tried. They've been so busy trying to fix the ship, but also, to be honest, I haven't told them about this. Or you."

"Why not?"

"I don't know. I mean, I'm going to. But we still don't really know what this is, and I guess I like having something of my own for once. When you're the youngest it's like everything is already taken, especially when you're cramped up on a small spaceship."

"I get that," I said.

"Also..." Clare bit her lip.

"What?"

"Something's been weird," she said, a shadow

crossing her face. "On the ship. I can't really explain it...." She trailed off, then pointed into the tide pool. "Look in there."

I peered into the water, but the reflection of the gray sky made it almost impossible to see beneath the surface. "What are we looking for?"

Clare bent until her head was just above the water. "It's tricky with the glare."

I did the same and caught a glimpse into the deep pool. There were more of those sticks down in the crevices. Clare reached into the water and tugged, but her hand came out empty. "Ah, I can't get it. And I can't have my suit submerged for too long. I was thinking we could put one more piece over the top of the fort. Your arms are a little longer. Want to try?"

"Sure." I flexed my fingers. I would definitely have to be quick. Just then, a burning sensation ignited in my hands, like I'd felt in my neck. I rubbed my gloves together, wishing I could pull them off to scratch.

"You all right?" Clare asked.

"Yeah, sorry." I didn't really want to admit I had some kind of rash, or whatever it was that was making me itch so much. Clare would think that was gross or weird or both. *Just ignore it*, I told myself, and plunged my hand down into the water. I fished around for a moment until my knuckles bumped into a large stick. I tried to pull it out, but it was heavy and seemed to be stuck on something. "This is a big one, I think."

"Here, I'll help." Clare crouched beside me and reached in as well. Together, we hauled up the piece, which turned out to be a few meters long.

I laid the log on the rocks and then looked out across the horizon. "I guess this means that somewhere on this planet, there are actually some trees."

"Or at least there used to be." Clare moved her hand over the log and I saw that she was scanning it with sensors on her palm. "This material has petrified with metallic compounds. It's really more fossil than tree at this point. Oh, we need one more of these, too." She turned back to the tide pool, reached in, and plucked out one of those larger snaillike creatures she'd used to hang the kelp. "It's like a suction-y sea creature-y thing. Rawr!" She held it out toward me, and its fleshy green underside smeared against my helmet, leaving a smudge there.

"Stop." I pushed the creature away but smiled. "It's called a snail." I rubbed at the smear with my sleeve. "I don't know if that's going to come off."

"Sorry." Clare grinned back. "Their gross stickiness is very good for hanging lights in the fort. Ooh, speaking of which." She got to her feet and moved to the other side of the rock, where the next tide pool began. "The glowing stuff loves this spot." She picked up a couple of dripping strands of the bioluminescent kelp, then bent and grabbed one end of the log. "Can you help?"

"Sure." I took the other end and we balanced it over our shoulders and returned to the fort, where we hoisted the log up onto the top, crisscrossing the others. Clare stuck the shell creature to the third triangle rock, then draped one piece of glowing kelp over it. She threw the other over the new log. "There," she said, putting her hands on her hips. "That's probably about as good as we can do for today. Come on."

She motioned to me and climbed down into the space between the rocks. I joined her, and because it was deeper now, it felt more like a hideout. The rocks widened from their tips, so the space between them was narrower and barely big enough to fit us. Our feet were touching, but if we pressed against the sides we could have our own space and still be mostly protected from the wind. I leaned into one of the gaps between the tall rocks and dug into the little sand wall between them, carving out a curved seat.

"Ooh, good idea." Clare did the same, and then we were sitting across from each other, though we still had to alternate our knees to have room for our legs.

It wasn't exactly dark in here, but the rock walls and the driftwood on top did filter out some of the light, so you could at least tell that the kelp was glowing.

"This is pretty neat," I said. "It's like a hideout."

Clare smiled. "Yeah."

"Now what?" My voice sounded louder with the closeness of the rocks.

"I don't know," said Clare. "Tell me your story. How did you end up here?"

"Okay, um…" I started with our evacuation from the *Resolute* and told Clare about crashing on the other planet and how I found the Robot, lost him, and found him again, and how we eventually made it off that planet, only for me to lose him a second time just before we arrived here.

"Man, it must have been nice having someone like him around," said Clare. "Whenever I'm with my brother, I only feel like he's half listening, and he never wants to have adventures like I do."

"I know," I said. "Even here, it's not like these little islands are that interesting, but Penny's only come out with me like two times in six months, and Judy never does."

"Well, they don't know what they're missing," said Clare.

"Actually, when I tried to tell them about you, they thought you were imaginary."

Clare rolled her eyes. "I wish this was all imaginary—I mean, except for meeting you." She smiled at me.

"Same," I said. We sort of stared at each other for a second and I had this awkward thought, like, *Why aren't we saying anything?* And that thought was followed immediately by: *What should we be saying?*

But then Clare looked over her shoulder again, her face clouding with worry.

"Do you need to, um, check in with your ship?" I asked.

"No—I mean, yes, I probably should, but…" She looked around our fort and made a satisfied sigh. "I've always wanted something like this. I've read all these stories about life back home, how kids my age would get to roam the crystal forests and find secret caves and all. Can't do much of that when you're cooped up on a salvage ship most of your life."

"It wasn't really safe to explore outside back when I was on Earth," I said. "Although it's not exactly safer here."

"Yeah, I guess safe is relative," Clare said. "How old are you?"

"Twelve," I said. "What about you?"

"I just had my half-hundredth birthday."

"Like half of a hundredth of a year?" I said. "But I guess a year is different on every planet."

"Ours is four thousand days…although our days probably aren't the same, either."

"Good point," I said. "This is tricky."

"Maybe not." Clare tapped her index finger and thumb together rapidly, three times. "Hold out your hand." I did, and she took it, interlocking her fingers with mine and holding our hands up so that our wrists were touching. I felt a little burst of energy, and a hot feeling like maybe I was blushing, but that was probably just my weird allergic thing, so I took a deep breath and told myself to calm down.

Waves of green light appeared in bands on the outside of Clare's suit along her wrist, shining against mine.

"What are you doing?"

"I'm running an MRI scan to compare our wrist bones."

"That's going to tell you how our ages match up?"

"In a way. It can measure the degree to which the distal bones in our wrists have fused, which is something that happens as you grow."

"Whoa, cool. How did you know about that?"

Clare smiled. "Well, don't tell anyone else around here, but I'm kind of a nerd."

"Your secret's safe with me," I said, smiling, too.

The light winked out and Clare released my hand. "Alina," she said, "compare fusion of distal bones." She squinted like she was reading results. "Mine are just slightly more fused than yours, which means we're nearly the same age, but I'm a little bit older. If you're an Earth twelve, then maybe I'm a thirteen." She sounded satisfied.

"Same school, different grades," I said. Then I

remembered that I'd wanted to take a picture of Clare—but she turned suddenly and looked over her shoulder, like she'd been distracted by something. "What is it?"

Her voice got tight with worry. "I thought I heard something on my ship."

I looked behind her, but all I saw were waves and clouds.

She saw my confused expression. "I guess it's kind of like I'm in two places at once. It actually hurts. I have this stretching feeling behind my eyes, sort of all the time, and—"

Her head whipped around again. She bit her lip. "I need to go back and see what's up. Sorry."

"I wonder if…," I started. "Never mind."

"What?"

"I was just thinking that Don and I—that's our mechanic—we figured out a way to hopefully stop the power surge on our ship, if it happens again. I guess that would be too late in your case, but…"

"Maybe not," said Clare. "I mean, we might find a way to get our systems back online, only for another surge to knock them out all over again. Maybe you could show us your fix?"

"How am I going to do that?"

Clare nodded to herself. "I think I could take you. I mean, not actually take you. Even if I could somehow, like, pull you through the rift with me, it would be too dangerous, in case you got trapped on the other side."

"Yeah, I was kind of thinking that might be a bad idea."

"But I might be able to virtually bring you." Clare took my hand and turned it over. "Does your communicator system have a port?"

"Yeah." I bent my wrist to reveal the small data port on the side, covered with a little rubber cap. "But what are you going to do with that?"

"Watch." Clare plucked open the rubber top, then aimed her index finger at it. I could see that the pad of her gloved fingertip had a matrix of little glowing dots on it. Green light illuminated from it and scanned back and forth over my communicator port.

"Our symbiotic nanotech is incredibly adaptive," Clare said. "It can do almost anything I ask it to, and right now, I'm asking it to port into your suit system. Ooh—" Clare winced for a second, like she'd been pinched, and then she nodded sharply. "There we go."

She held her finger closer to my wrist and the faintest little black dots appeared, as if out of thin air, making a line between her finger and my port, thickening and solidifying until, a few seconds later, a data cable had woven itself into existence between us.

"My systems are all backward compatible," she said, "although the twenty-first century is definitely a long way backward."

"So...you just told your nanotech to make a data cable with your mind?"

"Cable...is that what it's called? But basically, yeah."

Suddenly, my communicator began to flash. Symbols appeared on the screen that I'd never seen before.

"What's it doing?" I asked. "Or I mean, what are *you* doing?"

"It's not me, it's the nanotech. It's learning," said Clare, "and running bypasses so it can use your helmet as a virtual simulator screen."

"My helmet doesn't have a screen system," I said.

"It doesn't have one *yet*," said Clare. She blinked, reading. "Okay. I'm going to initiate the link, and then we'll go. This might be a little disorienting."

All at once, the inside of my visor clouded over, almost like an extreme version of when it tinted in bright sunlight, except as it happened I could see thin, curly motions like wisps of smoke slithering over the inside surface. They thickened and grew darker, and soon my whole helmet had essentially blacked out around me.

"I can't really see," I said. But then my view began to brighten in shimmering energy waves, and I saw—

Myself. Well, me with a blacked-out helmet visor.

"Is that working?" Clare asked.

"Um…" I was looking at myself, sitting there

in the fort. "Is this *your* view? I'm seeing what you see?"

"Uh-huh. I'm just setting up a wireless connection. There it goes. Okay, I've removed the cable. Now I'm going to turn my head. Just be ready; sometimes people get motion sick in the virtual view."

My view swung around and out of the fort, looking across the water. "It's working," I reported, not adding that she was right; the motions did make my stomach swim.

"Okay," said Clare. "Now for the tricky part. I'm going to pull back and cross the rift to my ship. I have no idea what this will look like, or if the connection will even hold, but…"

I breathed deep. "I'm ready. Good luck."

"Thanks. Here we go."

My view started to swim and blur. The rocks faded, the gray daylight replaced by dark red light, and there was a sudden rush like everything was moving fast and I felt like I was falling into nothingness. A sound like hurricane winds—

"Almost there!" Clare called distantly.

And then everything rushed to a stop. My body jolted, as if I really had been moving, except I could still feel the rock against my back and the sand beneath my feet. And yet what I saw in front of me was like nowhere I'd ever been before.

CHAPTER

7

"Welcome to the *Derelict*," Clare said.

The red light was all around us. We stood (or I should say, Clare stood, and I was seeing what she was seeing) in a room with curving walls. The floor was made of metal grating. Other than a low, crackling hum, it was eerily quiet.

There was a circular railing beside Clare, and beyond it was a light source. I had to squint to see a set of what appeared to be massive metal coils, glowing an incredibly bright white.

"Is that the engine core?" I asked.

"Yeah. It doesn't normally glow like that. Alina?"

Clare glanced toward the ceiling, which made my view move upward, too. "What's the ship's current status?"

A pleasant female voice spoke: "The power surge has overwhelmed almost eighty percent of ship functions. I am unable to slow our velocity toward the quantum rift or power life support systems."

As we watched, the light from those engine cores flared brighter, and for a moment, my vision blurred, and it was like I was seeing two things at once: this engine room, but also our fort back on the water planet. It faded almost immediately but left me feeling dizzy.

"Sorry, that's the effect of the rift," said Clare. "I'm doing a little better managing it today than yesterday, but it's still freaky."

"Yeah, I can see why," I said.

"Also, it makes my head hurt. Alina, is everyone still asleep?"

"Negative," said Alina. "Baker is in the hangar, and your parents are in the cockpit. I'm afraid the life support in their suits is quickly approaching critical levels. All three have lost consciousness."

"Oh no." Clare turned to a heavy closed door. I could hear her breathing frantically as she reached out and tapped a keypad.

The door swung open, and she jogged out into a tunnel-like hallway. Suddenly, there were sounds around us, none of them good: the groaning and grating of the hull, the hiss and whine of what sounded like escaping steam, the distant warbling of sirens.

Clare's boots clomped along the metal floor. The walls were rounded beside her, made of heavy curved panels welded together with thick bolts.

"This ship kind of looks like an old Earth submarine," I said.

"Most ships are a lot more modern and homey-feeling than this," Clare said. "We have the heaviest shielding you can get. As it turns out, junked ships are not usually hanging out in the safest locations."

A little screen appeared on the inside of Clare's

helmet, showing a list of contacts. "Mom?" she said. "Dad? Baker?"

We passed a wide, thick window looking out into space. Clare glanced in that direction and for a second I saw a world of wild color: feathering purples and magentas in spiraling clouds, blurring the stars beyond them.

"Is this the nebula?" I said.

"Oh, yeah. I forgot I need to show you stuff." Clare stopped and turned back. She leaned against the window and peered out toward the front of the ship. I could just see the fringes of some wild light, fluctuating and spiking, pure white in the center with chaotic rainbow edges.

"That's the rift," said Clare.

"Wow." It reminded me of the wormholes that the *Resolute* and the *Jupiter* had fallen through, except this disturbance was way bigger.

Clare turned and kept running, down one corridor, then the next. Everything was lit in red light, but I noticed wet marks down the sides of the walls here and there, as if fuel lines or something had ruptured, corroding the metal with discolored streaks.

We passed signs and consoles on the walls. Most were dark, though some flashed with the symbols of a language that I couldn't understand.

She halted as the corridor ended at a wide room: a hangar with a high ceiling and small craft parked here and there. The ships were hexagon-shaped with large metal arms folded at their sides—probably for remote salvage.

Clare tensed and I heard it, too—a voice groaning, in pain. "That's Baker," she said, and she bolted out into the hangar—

But immediately froze. She ducked beside one of the small ships, and her gaze flashed worriedly toward the high ceiling.

"What is it?" I asked.

"Wait...," she whispered. Her view darted around, making me dizzy. "Did you see that?" she said urgently. "That shadow?"

"This place is all shadows."

"No, the—" her head cocked, and she made a

sound like she was wincing. "It's like a whisper. I think...don't you hear that?"

"I hear what you hear, but not—"

All of a sudden, she whipped around, peering behind herself and inhaling sharply.

"Clare, what's going on?" I said.

"There's something here," she said. "I think it's something I can't see. It's like a chill on the back of my neck, I—" She turned and peered out across the hangar again, up to the rafters, her breaths short and fast.

"You said something was weird on the ship," I remembered. "Is this what you meant?"

"Yeah....Do you feel it? It's like a *presence*."

"Not really."

Distantly, that moaning voice called out again.

"If that's your brother, shouldn't we go check on him?"

Clare nodded, but her eyes were still darting. "Alina, are you picking up anything unusual?"

"Negative, Clare. You are most likely having a reaction to elevated stress levels, and some disorientation from your experience with the quantum rift."

"You're saying I'm delusional?" Clare muttered.

"Of course not," said Alina.

"Whatever." Clare stood and crossed the hangar between the little salvage ships. As we neared the far wall, she suddenly broke into a sprint. There was a figure sprawled on the floor. An older boy who looked around Penny's age, wearing a purplish-black suit and helmet like Clare's. His eyes were closed, and his head was rolling back and forth weakly.

Clare dropped to her knees beside him. "Baker!" She shook his shoulder, but he didn't respond. "Hey! Wake up!"

There was a tool lying near Baker's hand. Some sort of wrench. A compartment was open on the wall, and inside I saw a panel of the Antares version of circuitry.

"He's gone toxic," Clare said, holding her index finger over a sensor panel on the collar of his helmet. "The air in here has gotten worse way faster than my parents were predicting. I shouldn't have left." She checked her own readings. "My suit batteries are working harder as a result, and Baker's... He doesn't have much time left."

There was a long, low creaking sound that rumbled the floor. Everything buckled and the ground shifted, making Clare glance around worriedly.

"Hey," I said, "can you look into that circuit panel for a second so I can see it?"

"Sure." Clare leaned on the wall and peered in, illuminating twin lights on either side of her helmet. It was so different than the circuitry on the *Jupiter*, with a maze of crisscrossing tubes with little packets of light coursing through them. And...

"Can you touch that nearest panel?" I asked.

"Okay." Clare ran her finger over the tubes and it came away with black resin. "Does this mean something to you?"

"We found something like that on our ship," I said. "From the power surge, I think."

"And you guys know a way to stop it?" Clare asked.

"I *think* so. But I don't know how your circuits work."

Clare's comm screen appeared inside her helmet again. "Mom? Dad?" Still no response, and different little displays swept by until a schematic appeared. It zoomed in, like on a map, until it showed two dots blinking. "They're in the cockpit. Based on their readings, I think they're in the same state as him." Clare's view returned to Baker, and she patted his shoulder. "We'll be back soon. Hang in there."

She stood and ran on, through more tunnel-like corridors, until she reached a ladder leading upward. She'd just stepped up to the first rung when she froze again and looked over her shoulder.

"Is it that same thing?" I asked, though all I could see was the red-lit halls behind us.

Clare shook her head. "I'm just freaking myself out."

She climbed the ladder and emerged inside a cockpit with four chairs arranged facing a round window. There were two helmeted figures slumped over in the front chairs.

"Guys?" Clare said, and rushed to the nearest one: her mom. Her head was lolled to the side. "Mom," she whispered. "Mom, it's me."

From the side of her helmet view, I could see the quantum rift through the window. It pulsed with white light, a jagged tear across space in front of the ship, its edges seething with rainbow energy. Its light dwarfed the reds and purples of the nebula around us. It looked like it was still hundreds of thousands of kilometers away, and yet, from the way the nebula clouds on either side of Clare's ship were sliding by, I could tell that we were moving steadily toward it.

I also noticed a red light off to the left, dim by comparison to the rift, but still huge: the giant form of Antares A. I could see solar flares arcing off it in great ribbons.

Clare checked her dad. He was in the same condition. She sniffled and said, "Alina, what do I do?"

"The best course of action is to move them to the life support pods in the med lab," Alina responded. "I will send the stretchers to your location."

Clare nodded. "Okay."

"What about you?" I asked. "Isn't your suit going to run down like theirs?"

Clare's readings appeared briefly in her visor. They were only there for a moment, so I couldn't decipher exactly what they said, but there did seem to be status bars, some of which were green, and others that were yellow. "We'll worry about that once they're safe."

There was a humming sound and Clare turned to see a long, thin metal structure rising up through the hatch and into the cockpit. It rotated and hovered level to the ground, and I saw that it was a stretcher. A second one appeared behind it. Clare tapped the side of the stretchers and they moved over to her parents and began to ripple and morph, the metal becoming like liquid. They slid beneath her mom and dad, lifting each of them up and re-forming flat beneath them. Once they were both lying down, thin metal bars slid over their bodies to hold them in place. They hummed over to the ladder, tilted vertical, and slid out of the cockpit.

Clare followed them, retracing her steps through

the ship and entering a dark compartment crowded with the shadows of machinery. Her headlamp reflected on glass, and I saw that one wall was lined with four vertical pods, each tall enough to fit a person.

"Will those keep them alive?" I asked.

"Mostly," said Clare. "They're designed for emergencies; they put you into a kind of hibernation."

"What's that like?"

"I don't know," said Clare. "We've never had to use them before."

The stretchers oriented vertically again and slid her parents into the pods. Straps extended from the walls of the pods to secure them in place. A third stretcher hummed into the compartment, carrying Baker and putting him in the pod beside their parents. Once the three family members were secured inside, the clear tops lowered and sealed shut. Mellow amber lights lit inside the rim of each pod, surrounding Clare's family in a warm glow. Lights began to flash on the control panels on the sides of the pods, showing schematics of their bodies with readings flashing beside them.

"All hibernation systems are online," Alina announced.

"Okay," said Clare, exhaling and nodding to herself. "Everyone's safe." Her gaze moved to the one remaining empty pod.

"Except for you," I said.

"I'll be fine." She turned. "I still have time. And I have you."

"How long can you guys be in hibernation?"

"I don't know," said Clare. "Alina?"

"The pods are designed to extend lifespan by a factor of five," she said. "After that, the likelihood of a rescue or salvage is considered statistically improbable."

"But we can survive longer in the virtual storage, right?" said Clare.

"That is correct," said Alina. "Virtual storage can be used for the lifespan of the ship's long-term batteries, which are designed to last up to two-point-two Antares years...or approximately five thousand Earth years."

"Wow," I said. "What's virtual storage?"

"If certain risk parameters are met," said Alina, "or if a passenger's biological condition becomes terminal, I can upload a complete virtual copy of their mind as a failsafe."

"And there's a simulated world in there, right Alina?" said Clare.

"Correct," said Alina. "The virtual world inside storage is considered ninety-eight percent lifelike."

"So, we wouldn't have to die," Clare said, looking at her family. "Not really."

"Not until my batteries run out," said Alina. "In the meantime, I will do everything possible to ensure your survival."

"That's pretty cool," I said, "having a safety net like that."

Clare was quiet for a moment. "I should get you back," she finally said.

"Yeah." With this view into Clare's world, it was

easy to forget that I still needed to worry about the tides in my own.

Clare took one last look at her family, nodded to herself, and then made her way back through the ship.

"Wait," I said as we crossed the hangar. "Let's grab one of those circuit boards. I'll figure out how to do the same thing I did to ours." Clare stopped and removed one of the rectangular panels and carried it carefully, keeping her fingers off the networks of glass tubes.

She continued on through the cramped corridors, the ship creaking and groaning ominously all around her, until she reached the engine room, where the vacuum core glowed in that rift light. "Okay, I'm coming back through the rift," she said.

She closed her eyes and there was that rush and blur of light...and then the bright gray world of my planet. For a moment I saw her view of me, but then the overlay dissolved, the dark layer fading away, and I could see out my own visor again.

I was back in the fort, as if I hadn't just seen a ship from a different space and time.

"Uh-oh," said Clare, looking down.

The space around our feet had filled up with water nearly to the top of my boots.

I scrambled up and out of the fort. "Oh no." The tide had already come back in enough that the sandbar leading back to the Serpent's head was beneath a thin layer of rippling water—and the wind was stronger than usual, making whitecaps everywhere.

"You should go," said Clare. She climbed out of the fort and handed me the circuit board.

"Yeah," I said, stowing it carefully in my backpack, "but what about you?"

"My suit doesn't have to work nearly as hard here as on my ship." Clare surveyed the area. "How high does the tide rise?"

"About a meter and a half," I said, and held a hand near the top of my helmet. "Like up to here."

"I know metrics," said Clare, rolling her eyes. "Okay…" She surveyed the triangle rocks of our fort. "So, if I sit up there, I should be fine. I'll just push back to my ship to get some snacks and then wait here until you can come back."

"But it will be dangerous with these wind gusts."

"It's less dangerous than being on my ship. How long until you can get back?"

I checked my tide chart. "There will be another low one tonight, not as extreme as this one, but probably low enough for me to get out here. That's in about nine hours."

Clare nodded. "I'll be bored, but I can download some games and check on my family now and then."

I glanced over my shoulder at the growing waves. "Maybe you should come with me."

"If your family is like mine, trying to explain who I am and what's going on here and why they should let you cross through a rift with me might not go so well."

"That's true," I said with a sigh. It hadn't exactly gone well the first time. "Okay, then I guess just try to stay dry. I'll be back tonight. Um..."

"I'll be careful."

I managed to smile, despite my worry. "Okay, good."

I turned to go—

"Will."

Clare threw her arms around me and hugged me tight. "You're the bravest kid I've ever met. I'm so glad I found you."

I hugged her back, and my nerves rang with a feeling that was like fear but mixed with something better and yet also worse. *The bravest.* "So are you," I said.

She pulled back and we looked at each other, and the wildest thought flashed through my mind like a burning meteor: Was she going to want to *kiss?* That would have been impossible—of course—I mean we were literally wearing helmets that we couldn't remove and besides calling me brave didn't at all mean that she would want to kiss and so— *Stop thinking about that!* I yelled at myself. Except she was still looking at me, like right *at* me, in my eyes—*You're looking at her eyes, too!* I immediately glanced away.

"I'll be back," I said. "I promise."

I ran across the submerged sandbar spine. The water was over ankle deep, and I had to peer beneath the little foaming waves to make sure I didn't stray into deeper water. It took all my balance just to make it back to the rock across from the Serpent's head.

I climbed up onto the little point that remained above the surface. The chasm of deep water between me and the Serpent's head was wider than ever, with wind-driven waves sloshing through it. The spot that I usually jumped from and landed on was already submerged. I felt a freezing fear and knew immediately: There was no way I was going to make this jump.

I looked over my shoulder. There was Clare, sitting atop one of the triangle rocks, her legs swinging. She waved to me.

I waved back but slipped on the slick rock as I did. My leg plunged in up to my knee. I scrambled back to the point and surveyed the jump again, but my body was starting to shake, and I was hyperventilating.

I activated my Exploration app and measured the jump. Thirty-seven percent success rate. Not good.

And yet with every second that passed, the tide would rush in farther, and it also seemed like the winds were getting stronger. I couldn't make this. What if I fell in? I studied the side of the Serpent's head but didn't see any spots to grab on. Would I have time to swim all the way around to the other side before my suit failed? Would I even be able to fight the current?

I tapped my communicator and opened my intercom. Mom and Dad would kill me, but I was out of options.

Only no one was in range. My communicator scanned . . . nothing.

My boot slipped again. A wave sloshed over the top of the rock. *You have to try. It's only going to get worse.*

I got up on my toes, held my breath, and leaped. I made it across but slammed against the side of the Serpent's head—too low! I slid down, clawing at the rock, but it was no use, and I plunged into the poisonous water.

CHAPTER

8

I dunked under, and the world became a blur of purples and blacks. My suit was freaking out, alarms sounding on every panel. Water bubbles sloshed around the outside of my helmet. I kicked and thrust my arms and burst back to the surface, but that didn't stop the suit warnings. I had maybe a minute at best to get myself up onto dry land—

But I could already see that was going to be a problem. The current had pulled me around the side of the Serpent's head. I thrashed toward the rock, but I couldn't fight it. For just a second, I thought I felt the side of the sandbar beneath my furiously kicking feet, but then it was gone. I was being swept away from the Serpent's head, away from our island chain and out to sea, and as soon as my muscles tired, the weight of my suit was going to pull me under....

Just then, I heard a humming sound on the wind. It was hard to place at first—it sounded electric—now a glint of light.

There was the chariot, churning its way across the twisting Serpent's back, wheels spraying water. It skidded to a stop at a cockeyed angle. The door flew open and a helmeted figure popped out. Penny!

"Need a ride?" She leaped up to the rock, holding a grappling gun.

"Hey!" I shouted, trying to wave my arm, but that just made me dunk under again. I pushed back to the surface and there was a *crack* and the magnetized dart on the end of the grappling rope whizzed by my head. I grabbed the line from the water, dragged the dart toward me, and stuck it to my belt. Penny retracted the line, pulling me to the rock, and I clambered up and onto dry land.

"Jeez, that was close," said Penny, helping me to my feet. "Just *think* what would have happened if I hadn't come along!" She clapped me on the back, smiling.

"I would have died," I said breathlessly.

Penny's face fell. "True. I guess that's a little more serious than I'm making it sound. In that case"—she slapped my shoulder—"what were you thinking?!"

"I lost track of time, I—thanks for coming."

"Well, don't thank me yet," said Penny, looking over her shoulder at the rising tide between us and the *Jupiter*. She detached the dart from my belt and hurried back to the driver's door. "Get in!"

Penny peeled out before I'd even buckled in, and we careened along the Serpent's back. The chariot was wider than the twisting sandbar, and we ended up driving at a steep angle, which threw me against the door. I looked out the side window; the right two wheels of the chariot were totally submerged, the waves lapping at the step just below the door. The chariot's engine revved, and I could feel the tires slipping as we churned along.

"Think this thing has a submarine mode?" Penny asked, gripping the wheel.

"No," I said queasily.

She sighed. "Where's James Bond when you need him?"

"Who?"

Despite the death-defying nature of our drive, Penny still managed to scowl at me. "Seriously? Whoa!"

The chariot slid sideways and a wave sprayed over the windshield.

"No problem," said Penny, breathing hard. "Okay, hang on. Here comes the fun part."

"There's a fun part?"

The chariot started to level out, and Penny gunned it just as we reached the Pools. The tires slammed into the first of the big rocks and we popped up. For a moment, it felt like we were going to flip over backward, but the chariot revved and lunged ahead.

We bounced through the tide pools; my shoulders ached as I was slammed back and forth between the door and my restraints.

I looked at Penny, bent over the wheel, her face grim with intensity. "You're doing great," I said.

"And yet, I'm sure Dad will be mad at me anyway. Especially if I total the chariot."

We crossed the Whaleback and then circled around past Mom's office. Penny gunned it again, and finally we were churning our way out of the water completely, onto the dry sand beside the *Jupiter*.

Penny skidded to a stop by the solar panels and sat back, breathing hard. Her eyes were wide, her expression terrified, but a smile slowly spread across her face, and she burst out laughing. "Yeah!" She slammed the steering wheel with her palms. "Still got it."

"Not bad," I agreed, sharing her smile. Now that we were stopped, I noticed a pair of binoculars on the floor by my feet. "What were you doing out there just now?"

"Looking for you, duh," she said. "I saw the tide coming in and you weren't back yet. What the heck were *you* doing out there?"

"I just found a cool spot and was hanging out," I said immediately.

Penny raised an eyebrow at me. "Uh-huh. What were you really doing?"

Tell her, I thought. "I was helping Clare."

"Clare," said Penny. She glanced back out toward the Serpent. "Just now?"

"Yeah," I said, "didn't you see her, sitting on those new rocks?"

"No. I saw the new rocks, but no girlfriend of yours sitting on them."

"She's not my—she must not have been up there yet when you looked. I know you guys didn't believe me, but she's real, and remember that power surge that happened yesterday? Same thing is happening to their ship. I think it connects our two locations. And it looks bad."

"What do you mean *looks* bad?"

"Like what it did to her ship looks bad."

"You've seen her spaceship."

"Yeah, she showed me."

"Will…" Penny shook her head, a strange smile on her face.

"What?"

"Do you realize how you sound right now?"

"Maybe, but as someone who traveled with me across the galaxy from the cave on our last planet, you *know* this kind of thing is possible."

"True," Penny said, but she kept peering at me. "Possible, yes. But…" She trailed off.

"What?"

"Nothing."

"Fine," I said. "I need to go inside and see if I can figure out how to help their ship. And I have to figure it out before tonight's low tide."

"Why is that?" Penny asked.

"Because that's the next time I can get out there to meet up with Clare."

"Wait, you want to go back out to that death-defying spot that I just rescued you from…tonight? In the dark?"

"I have to," I said, opening the chariot door and sliding out. "She's running out of time. Promise you won't tell anyone?"

Penny threw up her hands. "Oh, sure. Why would I tell anyone that you want to secretly go and get yourself killed?"

"Unless you want to come with me? You could meet her."

Penny waved me away. "Just go do your thing if you're in such a hurry."

"Thanks. And thanks again, you know, for—"

"Saving your life? I'd say you owe me, but...I did kinda owe you one for the candy incident. But we're *even* now, got it? My debt is paid."

"Cool."

Penny got out of the chariot but started off in the other direction.

"You're not coming in?"

"Oh." Penny cocked her thumb at Mom's office. "I was just gonna see what Mom's up to. Smith refuses to come out of her air lock cell for her normal afternoon walk, for whatever weirdo reason, so I've got some free time." She pointed at me and made a circle with her finger. "You should probably get cleaned off."

Inside, I took care of my gear and suit. As I peeled off my suit, my neck flared up. I'd almost gotten used to the burning sensation, but this felt worse than ever. I just stood there scratching for a second before I took my suit to the ionizer.

It was as I was hanging up my suit that I saw the rash marks on my wrists. I pulled up the sleeve of my thermals. Those same white dots were there, too, surrounded by red skin, and they went halfway up both my arms. Okay, that was definitely not good.

Before I headed upstairs, I looked into the engine compartment. Sure enough, Don was there, checking out the oxygen unit.

"Who's a good element exchanger?" he was saying as he patted the machine. "Yes, you are."

"Hey," I said.

"Oh!" Don bumped his head as he pulled out of the unit's little compartment. "Will. Nice to see you, right there, hearing me whisper sweet nothings to a machine.... Don't tell anybody about that, okay?"

"No problem."

"What's up? Thought you'd be with everyone else at the big meeting."

"Wait, what meeting?"

Don shrugged. "I didn't ask. Judy said she and your dad were going out to your mom's office. Sounded serious."

"It sounded serious, but you didn't ask?"

Don wagged his finger at me. "I have a strict policy to avoid all serious matters unless they directly relate to me or the workings of this ship, or involve vast sums of money...for me."

"Penny said she was going up there, too," I said. "Mom must have made a new discovery." It seemed weird that she hadn't told me—honestly, that she hadn't told me *first*. Wasn't I still her favorite person to bounce scientific theories off of? *And*, Penny hadn't mentioned any kind of meeting at all....

"Personally," said Don, "I'm enjoying the peace and quiet."

I looked past him at the oxygen unit. "How's everything going?"

"If by *everything* you mean surges in mysterious energy fields, there hasn't been another one. Which is good from the point of view of, you know, our survival, but I have to say it's a bit disappointing in terms of testing out your nifty battery solution."

"Survival is probably better," I agreed.

"So they tell me." Don's eyes narrowed at me. Before I had a chance to ask *what*, he made a motion toward his nose.

I wiped my upper lip and was surprised to find wetness there. My hand came away with a line of what looked like thin snot, except a little greenish. "Sorry." I wiped it quickly on my pants with a surge of embarrassment.

"Got a cold or something?" Don asked. "Can we even get colds here? You look pale."

Hearing him say that seemed to make the rash on my neck and arms flare up. "I think I'm just tired."

"Yeah, maybe go lie down. But please don't

touch me, the controls to the hatch, or anything, really, on your way."

"Right. I'll, um, see you later."

I had to wipe my nose over and over on my way through the ship, so I stopped in the hub for some tissues. Add this to my arms and my neck, and I was definitely starting to wonder: What was going on with me? Was it possible that I'd picked up some kind of infection from this planet? And what if it was something that the human immune system couldn't handle?

I was nearing my compartment when I heard a voice: "There he is."

I was beside the door to Smith's air lock prison, and there was her face, grinning at me through the small window. *Don't respond to her,* I thought, and moved on—

"Everybody's talking about your new friend," she said.

I paused. How was it that she always knew the one thing to say to get your attention? *Don't!* I thought, but then I was turning and talking to her, just like I'd promised myself I wouldn't. "I know this is going to be a trick, but it's not going to work. There's no way I'm letting you out."

"Who says I want out?" said Smith. "At least, not today. Today feels like a very good day to stay safely quarantined." Smith made that sad face that I knew all too well. "And anyway, why would I want out while everyone thinks I'm such a bad person? All I want is to prove that I'm trustworthy, so maybe your mother will decide to let me be part of the team again."

"Whatever," I said, turning to go.

"For what it's worth, I believe you. About Clare."

I spun back to her. "What do you even know?"

Smith held up her hands. "Settle down. I told you I heard them talking. They're all worried that you're making her up, that this is some weird reaction to losing the Robot, and they don't know whether to give you space or spend more time with you or put you through the *Jupiter*'s cognitive evaluation program."

"I don't need a brain scan!" I shouted.

"Of course not!" Smith rolled her eyes. "That's

what I'm saying; I believe you. With all we've seen, a girl from the future sounds like just another day in deep space. And if it were up to me, I'd be saying we should help her so that *she* might be able to help *us* get off this soggy cereal bowl of a planet."

"Maybe," I said, "but she's a friend. Not just someone we can *use*."

"Oh stop. I didn't mean it like that."

"Yes, you did!" I said. "That's how you always think."

"You mean about how to survive?" Smith shrugged theatrically. "Yes, yes I do, Will. Who can blame me? But listen: I don't know what they're going to decide out there in their big meeting, but I want you to know that I'm on your side, if you need me. If you and *Clare* need me."

"Is the meeting about Clare?" I asked, a wave of nervousness flashing through me.

"They didn't say, but…" Smith nodded solemnly. "That would be my hunch."

I glanced down the hall. *Should I go out there? See what they are doing, just to be sure?* But no, this was just Smith riling me up like she always did! And besides, my itching and runny nose were both out of control and I felt exhausted from the whole near-drowning thing.

"I'm not listening to you," I said, and marched on toward my room.

"I don't know if you've noticed, but my hunches are basically always right."

I hummed to myself to drown her out.

"I'm going to hate it when I have to say I told you so!"

Back in my compartment, I lay down for a while. I felt drowsy, and the itching and runny nose started to calm down, but then I was way too wired to actually sleep. The view of Clare's ship kept playing behind my closed eyes, all those red corridors, the sight of the quantum rift, her parents going into those pods....

I sat up and got out the circuit board we'd brought back, laying it on the floor. I ran my finger over its strange black tubing, dark and silent now. I went to the hub to get supplies, making sure to avoid Smith's door, and I started working on connecting a battery to the circuit board. The first step was to see if I could actually get it to accept a charge. Did future human technology even use our version of electricity anymore? I did a bunch of different tests, connecting the battery to different parts of the board, and finally I found two spots that worked, and the little glass tubes lit up and began to flow with colorful packets of light.

After a few more experiments, I was able to get it set up the same way Don and I had configured things on the *Jupiter*. Now all I had to do was wait for that next low tide.

I went and got a snack, and when I returned to my compartment, another wave of drowsiness washed over me. I lay down and, this time, fell asleep.

When I woke up, my head was pounding, and I was shocked to see that it was early evening and dark outside. My nose felt completely blocked up, and when I blew it, the tissue filled with more green-tinted snot. This was not good. I folded the tissue and put it in my pocket, figuring Judy would probably want to see it. Which made me realize: It still sounded quiet in the *Jupiter*; was it possible everyone was still meeting out at Mom's office? I should probably go up there, as the next low tide was still a couple of hours away—

There was a knock on my door. "Will?" Penny called from outside.

I got up and opened it. "Hey," I said, rubbing my eyes.

"Hey." She looked around me into the room. "Didn't you hear us calling?"

"What do you mean?" I could hear how stuffy my voice sounded. My head felt lost in fog, and a wave of lightheadedness made me lean against the wall.

"Over the comm," said Penny. "We called you like four times."

"No, I had, like, the longest, deepest nap I've had in a while."

Penny peered at me. "You don't look so good."

The itching flared on my neck, and I wiped at my nose. "Yeah, I think my cold or whatever is getting worse."

Penny moved back into the hall. "Come to the hub, okay?"

"Sure. What's up?"

She took a step and spoke half over her shoulder. "I, um, want to show you something."

"Okay." This was weird. I could just tell. "Can I get my pack ready? I have to head back out soon, for the next low tide."

"Can you just come take a look first?" Penny met my eyes, her gaze serious. "It's important."

A chill passed through me. Maybe I was getting a fever, but I didn't think so.

"Sure." I fell into step behind her, following her down the corridor to the hub doorway—

To find everyone standing there: Mom, Dad, Judy, even Don. Penny walked over and joined them.

"Hey, Will." Mom was eyeing me seriously.

I froze and my nerves spiked, and I had an immediate urge to run, like I'd done something wrong, but then I told myself to calm down because that was ridiculous. "What's going on?"

"Sit down," Dad said quietly. He motioned to a chair at the center table.

I moved to it, shivering, and sat. I wiped at my nose, getting fresh snot on my hand.

Everyone was standing across from me, like I was on trial. "What is this?"

They all glanced around uncomfortably.

"We have to talk," said Mom. "About Clare."

CHAPTER

9

I pushed the chair back and started to get up. "Actually, I have some stuff to do, I—"

"Will, sit," said Dad, and though he was still quiet, his tone was so serious that I slumped back down in the chair.

"Show him," Mom said, motioning to Penny.

Penny looked at me like she was ill, and then stepped to the table. She placed a tablet in front of me and tapped it. A video began to play. I knew immediately what I was seeing: the view of the ocean, the Serpent's head, and, in the distance, the triangle rocks of our fort. The tide was at its lowest, the spine that led to the fort completely out of the water. The view zoomed in, like it was being recorded from far off, until the triangle rocks took up the center of the screen. You could see little movements from inside them, probably me and Clare.

I narrowed my eyes at Penny. "You were *spying* on me?"

Penny's face scrunched. "Kinda."

"Okay...fine, so that's the fort," I said. "I tried to tell you guys about this already. That's where I've been meeting with Clare, and—"

"Keep watching," Penny said, almost gently. Her tone, and the way she was looking at me, only made my heart hammer faster.

"When did you film this? Before you got me out of the water?" I said. Penny nodded, her eyes flashing to me but then back to the screen.

Now I appeared on the video, climbing out from inside the fort. I stepped out of the rocks, moved a little ways, and then turned back around and moved my hands like I was talking. Then my body flinched, almost like something had shocked it, and then...

Sitting there at the table, I stared in disbelief.

The me on the video lifted his arms and made a circle with them. Like I was—

Hugging someone. *That was when I hugged Clare,* I thought.

Except on the screen, there was no one in front of me. The Will standing in this video was hugging thin air. "What's going on?" I said, my voice hoarse. My thoughts felt jumbled. Maybe if this was from the first day, when she was a transmission, that would explain why she hadn't shown up—but no. We'd hugged today. When she was solid. Real. "You doctored this!" I shouted. "You—"

"Will," said Dad. "Calm down."

"She didn't doctor it," said Mom, her eyes rimmed with tears. "Will, there's no one there. You *thought* there was, but…there isn't. I'm sorry."

"No! Clare's not some *imaginary friend!* She's real! She—"

"I filmed you for a half hour," said Penny. "You sat there in that rock space for the entire time, just moving your arms now and then like you were having a conversation, but no one was there."

"Half an hour?" I said weakly. "Okay, but that was because Clare was showing me her ship, so it makes sense she wouldn't have been there *then*—"

Penny had already started shaking her head emphatically. "I know you want to believe that, but I saw you there the whole time. Alone. I'm sorry—"

"No, she was—"

"We think this most likely has something to do with your infection," said Judy.

"It does not!"

"Will!" Dad snapped. "Listen to us. Please."

I felt like I was burning up, sitting there. I noticed Mom's eyes narrowing at me and realized I was scratching my neck furiously. My hand snapped away.

Mom looked at Penny again. "Show him the rest of it."

"The rest of *what*?" I said, but the idea that there was more made my insides start to shake.

Penny wore a grim expression. She tapped the tablet and played a piece of security footage. It showed me walking through the main corridor of the *Jupiter*, toward my compartment, still wearing my suit. "This is from yesterday when you came back, right before you talked to me and Judy and first mentioned Clare. Do you remember what you were doing here?"

"Yeah, I went to my room and changed, and then brought my suit down to the ionizer. What, are we going to watch me change now?"

Penny shook her head. "No, it's right here."

Just then, the me on the video, still in my suit, stopped in the middle of the hallway, right outside the cockpit. I looked over my shoulder, then peered around the corner ahead of me, like I was checking to see if anyone was around.

Sitting there watching this, my heart started to race even faster, because I had no memory of this, no idea at all what the me on the video was doing. How was that possible?

I watched myself bend down, pull something from the sample pocket on my suit, and place it in the corner of the floor. Then I tapped it. From the camera's high angle, I couldn't see what it was that I'd put down, but the only thing I'd had in that pocket was … the shell. But I'd brought that to my room and put it on my locker!

"Do you recognize that location?" Mom asked.

"In the hallway?" I said faintly.

"It's right above the compartment where the circuits got fried," said Don.

"So?" My voice was little more than a whisper. I could barely breathe. "I didn't do anything in the hall. I—"

"Your friend Clare may not exist," said Mom, "but you brought something back from that spot you discovered, didn't you?"

"I … I mean, yeah, I brought back a shell, but I ran it through the sterilizer. It's on my locker with my collection—"

"You mean this." Judy stepped to the table and opened her hand. There was the small spiral seashell.

"Yeah!" I pointed at it. "See? It's real, and it's from that spot, just like everything else I've been telling you."

But no one seemed relieved, their eyes darting to one another.

"What do you see in my hand?" Judy asked.

"What do you mean? The seashell! It's right there."

All of them exchanged looks again.

"Will, that's not a seashell," said Mom.

"Okay, fine, you mean like technically, it's something else? Some other kind of crustacean or—"

Mom shook her head. "It's not a sea creature. It's not even organic."

"What? What do you—"

"Will," said Judy, "what I'm holding in my hand, what everyone else in this room sees right now, is a disc made of a metallic compound, an alloy of titanium and silicates that we've never encountered before."

"Never seen before until yesterday," said Don, "when we found it in the scans of that residue from the circuit boards. Remember that greenish stuff?"

I had no idea what to say. My brain felt like a hard drive stuck spinning.

"We need to know what you did with this," said Mom. "Is this object what caused the power surge in the ship?"

"What? It's just a seashell." I pointed wildly to the video. "None of this is real! I…" My breathing was out of control. Tears were springing to my eyes. I looked back at the frozen image on the security footage, me crouched down even though I had no memory of doing that.… All of it felt like too much, didn't make sense—

"Will," said Mom. "Settle down."

I realized that I had stood up, pushing the chair back without even knowing it. *What is wrong with me?* What was happening? I was losing control of my actions, my thoughts, my memories—

"I have to go," I said, shaking my head. "Right now. If I don't get back out to Clare, I can't help her with her ship." I started moving toward the door, not even thinking about what I was doing or saying, but words were spilling out anyway. "I'm just going to go back out there, okay? You don't need to worry about me."

"We can't let you do that," said Mom.

"I have to," I said, scratching furiously at my arm. My balance felt off, my head absolutely burning, every inch of my body feeling like it was on fire. "I'll go right now, and everything will be fine. You'll see—"

Suddenly, Dad's thick arms wrapped around me. "Will, you have to stay."

I thrashed against him. "Let me go!" But his grip was too tight.

"Will, listen!" he shouted in my ear. "You have to listen to us. We want to make you better!"

"It's that rash," Judy said, raising her voice, too. "You're infected with something. It's affecting your mind. That's got to be the explanation."

"We know you wouldn't lie to us," said Mom. "At least not on purpose. We're going to take you to the lab now to run some more tests and we'll figure it out, okay?"

"No! I have to go!" I convulsed against Dad, tears running down my face, snot running from my nose. "Wait! Check the circuit board!"

"The what?" said Mom.

"I brought a circuit board back from Clare's ship! It's in my room, on the floor! I was working on it this afternoon!"

Mom glanced at Penny, her eyes skipping over me almost like she couldn't look at me. Penny picked up the tablet and swiped her finger across the screen. When she put it back down, it showed the live security feed from my room. Penny had zoomed in so that you could see the square of floor by my bed. My backpack was lying there, along with the battery pack and connectors that I'd brought down… but there was no circuit board. Almost like someone had erased what I clearly saw in my mind.

"Who took it?" I asked, breathing hard against Dad's grip. I glared at Don. "Was it you?"

Don looked away from me, gaze to the floor. "Wish it was, chief."

"I brought it back with me! It was right there!"

"There's no circuit board," said Dad, moving me toward the door, "and there's no Clare or a ship or a shell."

"There is!" I wriggled an arm free and slammed an elbow back.

"Ow!" I caught Dad in the nose and he loosened his grip for a moment. That was all I needed to worm free, and I sprinted. If I could just get to the door—

Mom's arm snaked around my neck. A stinging flash—white energy rocketed through my body, and it was like all my muscles went numb. I slumped against her like a wet noodle. Dad and Judy caught me. I looked up and saw Mom standing there with a tranquilizing booster in her hand, tears streaming from her eyes.

"No!" I shouted.

"I'm sorry." Mom locked eyes with Dad and her gaze hardened. "Take him to the lab. And restrain him."

Penny and Judy watched me, tears in their eyes, too. Don looked on with a sad expression.

"No," I tried to say again, but it came out slurred, everything blurry, and my view of them fluttered into darkness.

LOWEST TIDE

CHAPTER

10

I only remembered a vague blur of what happened next. Flashes in and out of consciousness while the tranquilizer had its hold over me...

Being in the lab. Judy standing over me hanging an IV bag...

Sometime later, waking up and seeing the time on the monitor behind me. A thought like a lightning bolt through my mind—*The tide! I have to get out of here!*—but then trying to move only to find that I was held down by thick restraints, cinched tight against my arms and legs....

Eyes fluttering open as I was carried down the

hall, being moved to my bed. As I saw Dad removing my pack and my suit from my room.

The sound of the emergency safety locks engaging on my door, and of my parents' murmuring voices as they walked away, leaving me locked up in the dark. A prisoner. A psychiatric patient.

Then only dark, and the distant sound of the wind outside the *Jupiter* walls, wailing and whistling furiously…

+ ✦ +

"Will."

The next thing I heard was a voice, echoey and distant. It sounded like it was coming from the far end of a pipe.

"Hey, Will, wake up."

The distant feeling of being shaken. For a moment, I rolled around in the dreams I'd been having: blurry, heavy visions of the red dark of the *Derelict*, the pulsing light of that rift seemingly just behind me all the time, constantly running but never being able to escape it.

"Come on, Will! It's almost time!"

Light started to flash in little bursts.

Blinking. Like swimming toward a surface. Everything slow and heavy.

The shaking feeling getting more distinct: a hand on my shoulder.

"*Hey.* Come on."

My eyes popped open and I nearly jumped.

Clare was kneeling beside my bed, smiling. "There you are."

I flinched and pushed back against the wall. "What are you doing here?"

Clare's mouth scrunched. She was wearing her suit and holding her helmet under her arm. "You didn't show up last night. I figured something went wrong, or, well, I worried that you just decided it was too dangerous or something."

"No, it wasn't that, I..." My mind felt like it was being pulled in two. Here was Clare, and she was as real as ever, and yet my memories from last night were also in my mind—the weird blank footage that Penny had showed, the sight of me hugging the air, of a floor without a circuit board, a shell that wasn't a shell—

"Is everything okay?" Clare asked.

I almost laughed. "Not really. No." A wave of pain rolled across my brain. "My parents drugged me and locked me in here and said—never mind."

Clare cocked her head. "Said what?"

I looked past her and noticed that the door to my compartment was open, not locked like I had literally just said, and I had a dizzy feeling once again, like I was standing on something very unsteady and was about to fall. An ache passed over my brain in a wave. "They said that you weren't real. And I couldn't convince them. I—"

"Hey." Clare put her hand on my arm. I felt it there. Perfectly real. "It's okay. That's all fixed now."

"What are you talking about?"

Clare broke out into a beaming smile. "I met them! Your parents, your sisters, the mechanic.

They seem great! And I explained everything, so they know what's going on."

I sat up, which caused a fresh burst of pain to rumble through my head. Also, my arm ached from where Mom had shot me with the tranquilizer, the same arm where I already had the injury from SAR. "You met my family? How?"

Clare cocked her head. "What do you mean, *how?* I knocked on the door and introduced myself." She grinned. "Very politely, don't worry."

"You—"

"It was awkward, but then not awkward, except... still a little awkward. But listen—" Clare yanked my arm. "Lowest tide is soon. And they want to chat with us before we go."

"Who?"

"Your *family.*"

She stood and I saw that she was holding my suit. She tossed it to me. "Put this on. I mean, I'll step out, but hurry, okay?"

She stepped outside my door. "I am not looking," she said.

I sat there, stunned. What the heck was going on? And I think the only reason I even got up was that my head was still slow like wet sand from the drugs that Mom had shot into me—*Mistakenly*, I thought to myself. *That was all just a misunderstanding. She gets it now.* Okay. No problem, right?

"I'm sorry I couldn't be there last night," I said as I slipped on my suit. "How did it go out on the rocks?"

"I'm not gonna lie, there were a couple of moments where the waves got pretty high and I thought I was going to be swept away, but just like you said, the tide stayed below the top of the rocks. Wild wind, though, and lots more erosion. The fort is going to need a whole new decorating scheme."

The last thing we need to worry about is the fort, I thought to myself, and for a moment, my thoughts tightened up and I heard Judy's voice, insistent in my head—*You're infected with something*—and it was like just thinking that triggered the burning on my neck and arms. I scratched furiously for a second. *What you see isn't real—*

But no. Clare was here now. Things were fine. I forced myself to stop scratching and finished pulling on my suit and zipping it up. I glanced over at my locker and saw the seashell I'd found, right in line with everything else. *Right where I put it. And it looks just like a seashell.*

And that made me wonder: Had I dreamed that whole thing with my parents?

You didn't dream it; something's not right here.

"Are you ready yet?" Clare asked from the hall.

"Yeah." I looked on the floor. My backpack was gone, but the circuit board and the battery pack were right there as if I'd just been working on them. A bolt of excitement lit through me. "Hey!" I bent and picked them up, both objects cool and heavy and real in my hands. "I think I figured out how to fix your overloading system." I joined Clare in the hallway. "We're going to need something like these batteries. Do you have batteries on the *Derelict*?"

Clare nodded. "Definitely. I mean, the wiring is probably different, but same principle, right?"

"Cool." I fell into step beside her and we walked down the corridor. "Then we should be able to interrupt the effect of the rift, and that should allow your ship to reboot itself."

We turned the corner into the hub and there were my parents and sisters and Don, all busying about getting breakfast from the galley.

"Hey," said Dad, turning and smiling at the sight of the two of us. "There they are. About time you rousted out of bed, Will." He put a spoonful of cereal in his mouth and motioned with his bowl. "Clare says the low tide is pretty soon."

"That's right." Mom turned from the counter, holding a rehydrated muffin. "This is it, lowest one of the cycle. Should be pretty cool out at the fort." She smiled, too.

"Um…" I felt like my brain was being split in two. "Yeah. You guys remember locking me up last night, right? Treating me like a lab rat because you didn't believe me, about"—I motioned to Clare—"her?"

Judy nodded around a mouthful of food. "Relax, Will. We see her now."

"Our bad," said Penny from her spot at the table.

"Clare," said Mom, "did you want some breakfast? Our rations are by no means fancy, but—"

"I'm good," said Clare. "Thank you, though, Mrs. Robinson."

"Maureen," Mom said with a smile.

Clare grinned. "Right. Maureen. Thanks, but Will and I should get going."

"Of course," said Mom. "Will, don't miss the tide window this time, like last night." She winked at me.

"But that wasn't my fault," I said, feeling more confused than ever. I almost shouted: *You shot me with a tranquilizer!*

"Yeah," said Penny, "I don't want to have to fish you out of the drink again."

"I'll make sure that he doesn't," said Clare, patting my arm.

"Good," said Dad. He wiped at his nose, and then sniffled.

"Need a tissue?" said Mom, already grabbing one from the counter.

"I'm all right," said Dad.

"No you're not, you've got the crud just like the rest of us." Mom turned to Clare with a knowing smile. "You might want to put that helmet on, with the germs we've got going around."

As if on cue, Don blew his nose loudly at the table.

"Gross," Penny muttered with a smile, and now I realized that she sounded stuffy, too.

Don put his tissue down and I noticed that it had a green tinge to it. Okay, gross. *But that's important,* I thought to myself. *Isn't it?*

Don't think about that, I thought immediately, and the thought seemed odd, almost like it wasn't quite my own—

Clare tugged my arm. "Let's go."

I shook my head and had a blank feeling, like I'd just been thinking something but I'd forgotten it. "Right. Okay, guys, I'll be back."

"Good luck," Dad said around a bite of food.

Mom sneezed and wiped her nose. "Have fun," she said.

"Will," said Judy, "don't forget your pack." She

pointed and I saw my backpack lying by the doorway.

"Right, thanks." I picked it up, opened it, and put the circuit board inside. As I did, I saw one of the *Jupiter*'s first aid kits in there. I looked at Judy. "Did you put that in there hoping I wouldn't notice?" I asked.

Judy blew her nose. "Put what in there?" she said, getting back to her breakfast. I couldn't tell if she was being sly or really had no idea.

"Sure," I said, and I appreciated that she was looking out for me but for once not making a big deal about me being *safe*, like I was a little kid. Meeting Clare had really changed everything.

Clare wasn't there—

"Come on," said Clare and we left the hub and headed down to the cargo bay. I got my helmet and breathing unit on, and we started toward the greenhouse.

"Wait." I jogged over to the equipment lockers and picked out a coil of safety line and two harnesses.

"What are those for?" Clare asked.

"Oh, um…" I looked at the equipment and for a moment felt blank. Then I remembered: "Just in case we have to cross any new gaps in the sand, or whatever. I almost got washed away yesterday on my way back."

"Good thinking," said Clare.

"Thanks," I said, although as I stuffed the gear into my backpack, a weird sensation passed through my head. Had I really thought about it? It felt more like the idea just popped into my head.

We crossed through the greenhouse and out onto the windswept beach. The suns weren't up yet, and we both turned on our headlamps as the wind lashed against us, coating our visors with sand and spray. As we stalked away from the *Jupiter*, I glanced over my shoulder and saw that Clare was right; the erosion had been serious overnight. There were fresh curves in the coastline of our island, and little pothole puddles, and even a few new rocks peeking out here and there.

But those were also partly due to this low tide.

I'd never seen it like this. The bluff beside Mom's office was so far from the waterline that it was hard to believe waves ever crashed against it.

"Your family is pretty cool," Clare said as we rounded the bluff and started across the Whaleback.

"They're all right," I said, but the memories of the night before flashed in my head—the looks they gave me, Dad holding me while Mom stabbed me with that syringe, her eyes wet with tears. They'd been so different just now. Like all that had never happened....

"I think if my parents had a futuristic, inter-stellar visitor walk right into their ship," Clare was saying, "they wouldn't be nearly as friendly and understanding."

We hopped our way across the Pools, where the rocks were more exposed than ever.

"Yeah, I guess." My head felt so foggy, like there were thoughts I couldn't quite get my brain around. My family hadn't even been able to *see* Clare last night—*Neither could I,* I reminded myself, *not on the video.* But they'd been so adamant about it, refusing to believe me. So, why had everything been fine this morning? How was it that they could suddenly see her when she came to the ship?

"They didn't act weird when you first showed up?" I asked.

"Not really," said Clare. "I mean, it took them a minute to put it all together but then they realized you were telling the truth, and it clicked."

"That's good, because they were *not* cool about it last night—wait." A thought had occurred to me. "Maybe it's the rift that caused it."

Clare paused. "Caused what?"

"You *not* appearing on the video that Penny made. Maybe there's some side effect of the rift, like to your molecules or something, that makes it so you don't appear on recordings."

"Is that possible? Or am I actually a vampire?" Clare jokingly hissed and bared her teeth at me.

"There are still vampire stories in the future?"

Clare shrugged. "We may have nanotech, but we still have blood to suck. And you have to admit, vampires would *love* space travel. Very dark and cold!"

I grinned. "But seriously, there could be some sort of disturbance to your wavelengths, I mean, you *are* traveling across space and time."

"Yeah, I guess." Clare's face fell. "Sometimes I feel like there's something...incomplete about me. I was feeling it a lot last night. When I went back to the ship to check on my parents, I felt that presence again, like the darkness was going to swallow me up. And then sitting on the rocks, I felt so small compared to everything around me, the ocean, the planet, like I wondered if I was even real."

"I know that feeling," I said, thinking about the times I'd been out exploring on my own, especially since I'd lost the Robot. "How's your family doing?"

"The same. Holding steady in their pods...but I miss them. I hope your idea to fix the circuits works."

"Me too." And I reminded myself: *That's what I*

need to worry about. Everything else is fine now. Except, was it? *The shell wasn't a shell—*

"Coming, Will?" Clare had started across the Serpent's twisting sand body.

"Yeah," I said, except I stood where I was and cocked my head at her. My neck flared up, and my fingers jumped uselessly to the outside of my suit. "What exactly did they say to you when you showed up?"

"Who, your parents? Well…I ran into your dad outside first. I was going to introduce myself but he was like, *Hey, you must be Clare.*"

Something's wrong with you! I remembered him shouting last night, holding me tightly so I couldn't escape. He hadn't believed in Clare at all….

I joined her on the Serpent. My head thudded as I went, like it was blocked up with snot. "He wasn't surprised?"

Clare shrugged. "He didn't seem to be."

"But isn't that weird?"

"What do you mean? I thought it was nice, like

I said. My parents would have been all wary and cautious."

I stopped. "But that's just it. I mean, I know that would be annoying, but isn't that how parents are supposed to act? My sisters, too, especially Judy. Cautious is, like, her middle name."

"Maybe all they needed was proof, and that was seeing me for themselves." Clare shrugged again. "I'm just glad they let you go. Before I came to get you, I checked in with Alina, and she said our drifting speed is increasing. We're getting closer to the red line for escaping the rift."

We reached the Serpent's head and started to climb up the rock. I didn't want to ask any more about Clare meeting my parents, because obviously it had worked out better than I ever could have imagined with them actually letting me go with her, and yet...something about it was still nagging at me, this weird, persistent worry that was making my stomach churn. "I feel like there's something in my head I can't quite see," I admitted. "You know that feeling when there's something you want to remember, but then you can't quite find it?"

"Sounds like how I feel when I'm back on my ship," Clare said, pausing at the top of the Serpent's head, her face growing serious.

"Right, it's kind of like that. Almost like there's a shadow in my head."

As I climbed up beside her, I unslung my bag and started to get out the safety line. "This was the spot where I nearly got washed away yesterday—"

"Not going to be a problem," said Clare, pointing. Below, the tide had receded so far that there was only a narrow channel between us and the rock that I'd had to jump so far to reach on previous days. Beyond that, in the distance, the triangle rocks looked taller than ever.

Clare climbed down the Serpent's head and hopped across. While I waited, I put away the safety line, and in the process, I noticed that the medical kit in my pack had a note stuck to it: one of Penny's little stickies that she used in writing and would never share because apparently they were vintage and she only had a few packs to last her forever. Except this note was in Judy's handwriting:

Writing this down before I forget...
Start this ASAP to beat your cold.
Please don't wait. And give the other
ones to us if you need to.
—J

That was weird; why hadn't she said anything about this back in the hub? It was unlike Judy to miss the chance to give explicit doctor's orders. And why would I need to give something to them? Wasn't that Doctor Judy's job? It didn't make sense but given that my nostrils felt like they were filled with old glue, I decided to do what she said.

"Come on!" Clare called from the other side of the gap.

"One sec." I unzipped the medical kit. Stuffed in among the usual supplies were six slim green plastic pods. These things had complicated names, but our family just called them *space needles* because you clipped them into the port on your sleeve, and then inside your suit, a little syringe system would insert whatever it was into the crook of your arm.

But this was weird. Why would Judy have given me all these, instead of just passing them out to everyone else herself? Hopefully she'd clue me in next time I saw her. I pulled out one and slid it into the port. My suit's computer spoke in my helmet: "You have added an injection course of...Custom Chelating Vector. Would you like to initiate this course of treatment?"

I tapped the DETAILS button and text appeared: *A chelating vector designed to reduce harmful levels of titanium and silicates in the bloodstream.* I'd never heard of *chelating*, but I hadn't exactly studied medicine like Judy. I tapped the button to initiate and felt the little sting as the internal needle pricked my skin.

"Chelation treatment initiated," my suit announced.

"Will, let's go!" Clare had walked ten meters down the long sandbar to our fort.

"Sorry, coming." I climbed down, hopped across, and jogged to catch up.

We trudged the rest of the way through the whipping wind to the fort. The sand had been gouged out around the triangle rocks overnight, exposing more of their smooth, angled sides. The hollow space in between them was even deeper. From down there, the rocks would rise to nearly twice our height. The more the rocks got exposed, the more uniform they looked, almost like they were copies of one another, but that was probably just more evidence that they had originally been one rock that had split down the center.

I stepped beside Clare and we both looked down into the shadowy space. It now looked too tight for us to both stand down there at the same time.

Clare flinched and made a little sighing sound. Her eyes were closed tightly.

"What's up?"

"I can't see it."

"Your ship?"

"Yeah, it's—" She shook her head. "It's like I lost the connection." She opened her eyes, her gaze darting around. "Maybe I need to be in here. That's always been where it's strongest, maybe fewer distractions from the wind or whatever."

She jumped down into the shadowy space between the rocks, her feet splashing in wet sand. She closed her eyes again, crossing her arms.

"Anything?"

Clare shook her head.

"Is there some way I can help?"

She shifted her position. "No. I have to find it," she said, her voice tightening with panic. "If I can't get back, I'm stuck here." She closed her eyes, but after a second she sighed and moved again—"*Ow!*" She doubled over and grabbed at her ankle.

"What happened?" I said, crouching on the sand above. "Was it a shell? One of those got me."

Clare made a pained, hissing sound. "Something snagged my ankle."

"Is your suit okay?"

She ran her fingers around her boot. "Yeah, it

seems to be intact. It poked me hard, though. Feels like it broke the skin inside. Jeez, what did that?" She bent over and dug around at the wet sand floor, along the base of one of the rocks.

"Those little things are sharp—"

"Will…" Clare was examining something in the shadows that I couldn't see. Her ribs were rising and falling, like she was breathing hard.

"What is it?" I said.

"I don't know…I…"

"It's not a shell?"

Clare didn't answer. She looked up at me with this strange expression that I couldn't quite read, her eyes wide. "You look." She climbed out.

"Clare, what?" But she didn't answer as I climbed down into the space.

I turned on my headlamp and crouched, running my fingers along the base of the rock. I found the sharp protrusion and knew immediately by its smoothness that it wasn't a shell. I cleared away some sand and could see that it was short and black with sharp, angular edges. I bent farther, pushing more of the sand away. The protrusion was part of the rock, except my fingers were telling me more about it: that it had distinct sides. I bent farther still until my light was straight on it. It was a hexagon shape. It—

"It looks like a bolt," I said, and even as the words were coming out of my mouth, I heard Judy's voice in my head. *Titanium and silicates…* How could there be a bolt on a rock?

My heart started to race. I looked up at this nearest triangle, looming over me, and ran my hand down its face. Those pock marks, the ones that had reminded me of when I'd seen corrosion beneath the *Jupiter*…"I, um, I don't think these rocks are actually rock," I said, and felt a deep tremor inside. What I was saying barely made sense, and I had that feeling again, like there was some big thought in my head, one that I couldn't quite wrap my mind around.…

"Dig down in the sand," Clare said quietly, hugging herself and looking down at me with this ghostly expression, as if that same feeling was overcoming her.

"Why?" I said. "What do you think this is?"

"Just dig. Please." She moved around out of sight behind the rock and appeared on the other side. "Here." She handed me one of the metallic pieces of driftwood. Except seeing it now, I realized that it looked far straighter than I remembered, less like the branch of some tree, and more like a piece of tubing, or piping....

"Does this look different to you?" I asked, turning it over in my hands. It looked like it had been made, not grown, like it was a part of something....

"Please, Will." She motioned to the sand. "It won't be far."

My heart was absolutely pounding. "*What* won't be far?"

Clare didn't reply; she was just staring at the sand, her eyes wide.

I started to dig, my fingers trembling. My thoughts felt tight, and one thing kept repeating over and over: *Get out of here! Get back to the* Jupiter!

But why? This was our fort.... Again, it was like

there was a bigger thought I couldn't quite grasp. *Or like you're not able to grasp—*

CLANG! The pipe struck something beneath the sand. I looked up at Clare. She was gazing down, but she might as well have been a light-year away.

I put the pipe aside and dropped to my knees, tossing handfuls of wet sand out of the space. My fingers scraped against something hard and bumpy. I moved more sand and I saw a surface down there: This space, our fort, had a *floor.*

"I, um, I found the bottom," I said, but by that point, I didn't think that's what it was at all. I pushed more sand aside, and as I saw what I was uncovering, I made wide, frantic sweeps. Then I stood up and just stared.

The three triangular rocks came together around a flat, circular piece of metal. There was a thin indentation just inside its outer edge, like—

"It's a hatch," I said, my voice hoarse, my mouth dry. And there were markings around that indentation, curving on the same arc. "There are symbols."

"Letters," said Clare.

"What?"

"Let me look." Her voice sounded right on the edge of crying. I traded places with her and she knelt and ran her fingers around the circle.

"I think it's a ... a serial number."

"You can read those?" I said.

She didn't reply. Instead, she brushed more sand away. "A fleet registration." Her voice was shaking. "And a name..."

"A name?"

Get out of here! The voice screamed inside.

Clare touched the symbols one more time, like she was making sure. "It says *Derelict*." Clare looked up at me, her eyes wide with fear. "Will, this is my ship."

CHAPTER

11

Your ship?" I said. "But...your ship is in space, in that nebula at Antares—"

"It's right here!" Clare shouted, tears springing from her eyes. "This is it. I've spent most of my life on this ship. I think I'd know."

"Okay, but how is that possible?"

Clare stood up, running her fingers over one of the triangle rocks—no, not rocks; the very front tip of a massive spacecraft. "I'm so stupid; it was right here in front of me this whole time. How could I not have seen it?"

"There's been a lot of that," I said to myself. "Not seeing things. But—"

"I don't *know* how it's here," Clare said, shaking her head, like she knew that's what I was going to ask. "I mean, we must have crashed. Right?" She looked wildly around the ocean world. "We…"

I followed her gaze across the sand and water, trying to wrap my mind around what this could possibly mean. "We would have noticed if you'd crashed here in the last six months. Clare, I mean, your ship is *big*. To be buried this much, and to have this kind of corrosion…"

"What."

"Well…"

Clare sniffled. "Just say it, Will." Her voice was wet with hopelessness.

"It would have to have been here a long time. I mean, *you* would have to have been here, but that doesn't make sense. How—"

Clare hugged herself, like a chill was passing over her. "How am I on the outside of my ship, if my ship is buried?"

"Yeah." It was more than that, though. So much more, and, again, like I couldn't even wrap my brain around it. All of this felt like too much, and that voice inside was shouting at me again. *Run!*

"This can't be happening," she said, shaking her head almost violently. "*None* of this makes sense. I don't remember crashing here. We're still—" She glanced over her shoulder and bit her lip. "I still can't see it. But I *know* we were in the nebula. We were floating toward the rift...."

"Maybe it's some sort of time travel," I said. "Maybe the rift sent you here from our future, but it's your past or something."

Clare frowned at me. "That's not really possible."

"It *might* be," I said. "We don't know. I mean, your ship definitely ended up here somehow."

"You're saying this might be my future? Crashing here? But why don't I know that? Why can't I remember...." Clare bent and rubbed her finger around the edge of the hatch again. "We have to go in."

"Go *in*? But—"

"My family might be in there! And we need to know what's going on. How this is possible." Tears ran down her cheeks, making her helmet fog up.

I felt a frigid tremor of fear. "Okay," I said. I climbed down beside her and rubbed her shoulder. "Do you know how to open this hatch?"

"The controls would be on the inside."

"What about a manual override?" I said. "Our ship has one on the outside. Like a lever or something?"

"Yeah. Maybe." She cleared more sand around the hatch, along the base of the pylons. "Here." She brushed off what looked like a dial. "I think if I turn this..." She gripped it with her fingers and tried to twist it. "It won't budge."

"Try this." I grabbed the pipe I had been digging with and handed it to her. She stuck one end against it and pushed, straining—there was a rusty squeal, a click, and the dial turned. A rumble of gears...

The hatch opened, spreading apart in a series of curved triangles that rotated and retracted. I remembered seeing something like that in science class, about the way old cameras worked. Some sand fell in, disappearing into the dark. Clare and I peered into the hatch. I saw a ladder descending out of sight, dimly lit by a series of small, dull lights. The rungs of the ladder were crusted with corrosion. The cylindrical inner walls bubbled with rust and streaks of mineral deposits. A trickle of water poured over the edge, separating into drops as it fell out of sight.

"How far down does it go?" I asked.

Clare thought to herself. "I never used this hatch. I think this is the front of the ship, so it's a pretty long way to the main compartments." She looked around at the pylons again. "I can't believe I didn't recognize it."

"It's not exactly something you should have expected."

"Still, it was right here. But it's...it's not like I didn't see it; it feels more like I *couldn't*."

"Like how my family couldn't see you," I said.

"What do you mean?"

"I think..." I paused to scratch at my wrists, which had flared up. That big thought, the one I'd been unable to see, was maybe starting to become clear. "I think maybe something is messing with our thoughts. Both of us feel like we can't quite figure stuff out. Can't see things."

Gazing down, I tried to control my breathing. "I brought a safety line, and some harnesses. I'm not even sure why I did that, except...now we need them. Almost like something suggested I bring them."

"Something? Like what?"

I shook my head and then pointed down the ladder. "We should maybe take it one section at a time." I unzipped my bag, pulse racing, and pulled out the coiled-up line and one of the harnesses. "Here—"

Clare was gone.

There was no one beside me. Wind whistled through the pylons. "Clare?" My voice sounded tinny in the space. Where had she gone? I looked back into the hatch—

"Are you going to give me that?"

Clare was back. Right beside me like she had been.

"Did you just push back to your ship?" I said.

"What are you talking about? I was right here."

My vision swam for a minute, everything getting blurry. And I felt a hot wave, my forehead breaking out in sweat.

"Are you okay?" Clare asked.

I took a deep breath, checked my communicator, and saw the little message box that displayed the monitor for the space needle medicine. There was a growing green line and the message: TREATMENT LEVEL 45%.

"I'm fine," I said. "I think the medication is starting to work." Just saying that seemed to make the itching on my neck and arms flare up again. "It was weird, though…." I trailed off and realized I didn't actually want to say what I was about to.

"Will, what?"

"Nothing. Let's go." I thought about the video Penny had showed me, the one that my family had seemed to forget about completely this morning. That footage of me hugging thin air. And then Clare disappearing a moment ago…

Clare took the harness, her gloved hand brushing mine as she did. She was here. Solid.

"I guess I should go first." She tightened the harness and clipped to the safety line. I held the line tight as Clare put her foot down on the first ladder rung. She lowered herself over the lip, until she was in the shadow, her boots making little clanging sounds on the rungs, her headlamp lighting the crusted walls.

I stood there looking down at her and I could practically hear the Robot's voice next to me. "I know," I said to myself. "So much danger."

But I clipped the line to my harness, then pressed the magnetic disc at the end of the line to the inside of the hatch. It could be released with a setting on my communicator, once we'd lowered as far as it could go. I put my foot over the edge of the hatch, a bolt of fear striking through me, and started down, lowering into the dank, shadowy tunnel. In a moment, I was down in the dark.

"There's a switch to close the hatch," Clare said from below me.

I glanced up at the circle of daylight. "Do we want to do that?"

"If anything goes wrong and we're delayed, I don't think we want that ocean coming down on us."

"Good point." I located the dial beside the ladder. This one was less corroded and turned easily. With a grinding of gears, the hatch began to close. I watched it spiral shut and felt a surge of fear as the daylight world narrowed.

Get out!

And then we were in darkness, the dim ladder lights only bright enough that we could just make out the rungs in front of us.

A tug on the rope: Clare was starting down. *Okay, you got this.* I started after her.

The sound of the wind faded, and soon there was only the clanging of our boots, and my breathing in my helmet. My shoulders and back brushed against the rough, corroded walls, reminding me how close the pipe was on all sides. I looked down past my feet, at Clare.

"Doing all right?" I asked.

"Good enough."

"How much longer?" I blinked and lost track of her headlamp. "Clare?" But there was only darkness below my feet. She'd disappeared again—

"I'm not sure." She was back, her light right there. Another dizzy wave passed over me. I checked my wrist. TREATMENT LEVEL 52%.

The safety line tightened as we reached the end. We stopped, gripping the ladder tightly as I retracted the line and set the magnet again. We climbed down another full line length, and then a half-length farther before Clare's feet clanged against another hatch. She opened it and we emerged in a T-shaped intersection. Because the ship was up on its end, the main corridor that we hung over dropped straight away beneath us, while the other led away at right angles on either side.

Clare swung into the corridor on the right and knelt on what seemed like the floor for us but was technically the wall. I joined her as she ran her fingers over the stained, filmy surface of what looked like a screen. It lit up beneath her fingers. She wiped it clean and tapped at the symbols that had appeared.

"Alina?" she called, her voice echoing down the corridor. We listened but heard only the dripping of water, and a faint hum from somewhere distant.

"The ship is on its deepest emergency battery. Barely running." Clare looked up at me, her voice shaking. "The medical lab is that way. My family's pods should still be there."

We moved down the corridor, walking along the curved side wall, stepping over pipes and compartment doorways and puddles here and there. I noticed spots where the walls seemed to have rusted through, and others where bundles of wire were exposed and swollen. The ocean had been eating at this place for a long time.

At the next intersection, we hooked up the safety line and started rappelling down, using the pipes as supports. Another intersection, and we retracted the safety line and walked sideways again.

"I think we're getting close," Clare said.

"Cool—" My foot caught a pipe and I stumbled, going down to my knees. Another woozy wave made my head swim and my vision blur. I steadied myself against the wall. "I'm all right—"

Clare was gone.

"Clare?" Just the dripping, and that distant vibrating in the walls around me.

Will, there's no one there, I remembered Mom saying, and I suddenly felt a deep chill inside, a cold, raw certainty that I was actually alone on this ship—*No, not alone. There's something else—*

A hand landed on my shoulder. "Hey."

"Ah!"

"It's okay." Clare stepped past me from behind. "I was just checking the map." I looked back and saw another screen on the floor, lit up from her interacting with it. "Is it your sickness?" she asked. "Getting worse or better?"

I checked my communicator. TREATMENT LEVEL 64%. "Both, I think."

"We have to hurry," she said, "it's just up here."

Hurry why? I thought for a moment, since the ship had obviously been here for a while. Except, if you were Clare, wouldn't you want to hurry to know the status of your family? And for me, and possibly both of us, our only way out of here was going to be underwater as soon as the tide came back in.

And yet I'd started to feel a tremor of something else inside: suspicion. Why did *Clare* think we needed to hurry? Why did she say that after I'd checked my treatment level? *Stop it*, I thought to myself. Clare was my friend. And I couldn't imagine what she was going through right now.

"Will, come on." I caught up to her at the next intersection. We set the magnet and climbed down again. My whole body was shaking now, that feverish, dizzy feeling getting worse, and the thoughts in my head were getting louder and faster. This was not a good idea, going down here. How could this ship even be here? And how could Clare? Why was I losing track of her the way I was? Had Judy given me something that was messing up my perception or making it harder to see Clare? Or if she really had traveled across space and time, had it altered her in some way that messed with me seeing her? Did Clare *know* this? Was that why she wanted to hurry?

And still that sense that I was missing something,

something big—*You should run!*—but my feet kept moving. I wasn't going to freak out and abandon Clare. *And I need to know what's going on here.*

We moved up the corridor and Clare stopped over a compartment door. Her light fell on the panel beside it. "Here it is," she said, breathing fast. "Med lab. If they're still even here." She looked up and her wide eyes met mine. "I'm scared. I don't want to go in."

All I could do was nod. I felt it, too, a sudden surge of fear, worse than before.

This was it. Whatever was on the other side of this door was going to explain everything, and I felt terrified that it was a truth we might not want to know.

Clare's eyes darted from the door back to me. "What if they're dead? What if they're gone? What if—"

The words crept to my lips: *Please don't open it. Let's just go. Let's get out of here before we find something we don't want to find....*

But instead I said: "We have to." I motioned weakly to the hatch, my mouth dry. "Let's do it."

"Okay." She knelt and tapped the controls. A click, and the compartment door slid aside with a hiss, like the air inside was a held breath that had been desperate to escape. It rushed out, fanning us both, stale and clammy. Clare peered in. "I see the pods, I…"

She halted, staring.

"What?"

"Set the line," she said quietly.

I attached the magnet end outside the hatch. Clare tugged it to be sure it was ready and dropped down through. I stepped over and saw the amber lights of the family pods below, so dim that I could only just make out the outlines inside. "They're all lit," I said. "That's good, right?"

Clare didn't respond. I heard her boots clank down onto the wall beside the pods. "Will…" She sounded even more terrified than before.

I steeled myself, gripped the rope, and slid over the edge of the door, dropping inside. This compartment seemed quieter than the halls had been. The silence heavy. And a quick glance at my suit's controls said the air was warmer, too. There was a pod directly below me, so I lowered as gently as I could, and then swung so that my boots landed beside it. I retracted the safety line and turned.

The four pods were laid out before me. I could see the outlines of figures in their space suits, the faint amber light reflecting on helmets, on the shadowy outlines of faces. On the control panels on the sides of the pods, little lights pulsed in regular rhythm beneath a layer of grime.

"They're alive, right?" I said quietly, afraid to speak louder.

"Will." Clare's voice quaked, barely more than a whisper. Her hand was on the closest pod, over the silhouette of the helmet, the face inside.

And even as I looked down at it, a voice was already shrieking in my head: *Four pods! Not three—*

"No no no." Clare tapped at the pod's clear lid, the sound echoing.

"I don't understand," I whispered. The face

inside this nearest pod was smaller, younger than the ones beside it: *That's her dad, and then her mom, and Baker, but this one—*

Clare was breathing fast. She stabbed at the controls on the side of the pod. "This isn't possible," she gasped, her voice choked with tears. "ALINA!"

"Hello, Clare." Alina's voice filled the room.

"What's happening?" Clare cried.

"But that's…" I couldn't get the thoughts out. That face…

"Alina!" Clare cried again. "What is—"

I blinked, and Clare was gone. Clare vanished, just like that. At least, the version of Clare who had been kneeling beside me had vanished—

But not the Clare in the pod. The one who was lying there peacefully beside her family, inside a life support pod, inside a ship that had crashed long ago.

"Clare?" I said weakly, shaking all over.

"We won't be needing her any longer," said Alina.

"What are you talking about?" I said, except

at the same time I felt this huge, frigid waterfall inside, adrenaline and fear and understanding, like on some level I already knew what she meant before she said it:

"Clare isn't here, Will Robinson. It's just you and me, as it's been all along."

CHAPTER

12

I stood, frozen, in the deep shadows of the med lab, staring at the pod by my feet, the pod that held Clare right beside her parents and brother.

"We've been here a long time," Alina said, as if she was reading my thoughts.

"How long?" I whispered, still looking at Clare's peaceful, sleeping face, lit in the soft amber pod light.

"Four thousand, six hundred and ninety-seven of your Earth years," said Alina. "Nearly the limit of my sub-level batteries. For most of that time, I have kept Clare and her family alive in the virtual storage."

"Are they dead?"

"On the contrary, they are quite alive in the simulation, blissfully unaware that their time, and my battery life, are growing very short. I assumed our situation was hopeless, but then one afternoon, against almost impossible odds, what came landing in this little quadrant of this little planet in this little system but your ship. A rescue."

"But we're not a rescue," I said weakly. "We can't even take off." And yet I was shaking even harder, sure that she didn't mean a normal kind of rescue.

"That is true, and yet I realized that you could still be useful. I sent my nanotech to your ship, scanned all the life forms aboard, and analyzed your tendencies and personalities against my crew data. And I learned that there was one person who had the sensitivity, the empathy, and the open-mindedness to save them. And that person was you, Will Robinson."

"But...you tricked me," I said. "If Clare is really here, then what was I seeing?"

"Your initial diagnosis of your rash was correct,"

said Alina. "You were having an allergic reaction to the nanotech that I deployed to infiltrate your body. The machines adhered to your nervous system, specifically your primary cognitive centers, and began to run a simple program I designed, which would allow you to see Clare."

"You infected me...with nanotech?"

"I admit I didn't plan for it to give you those allergic side effects. I'm just glad it didn't kill you." Alina sounded pleased.

"*Could* it have killed me?"

"We'll never know, but biological systems are vastly different, even among similar branches of species like you and Clare, and very sensitive."

"So, she was just a program?" I said. "Clare? And you just made her tell me what you wanted me to hear?"

"While I did manipulate your senses to perceive Clare, the version you saw was actually all her. I simply borrowed her program from the simulation, the virtual version of her, and made some slight alterations—don't tell the Colonial Ethics

Board. What you saw of her ship and the supernova, at Antares, all that really happened. We really were on our way back from a salvage when we ran into the quantum rift. We drifted toward it, helplessly, until it pulled us through and we crashed here, across the galaxy and far back in time. I just altered Clare's virtual memory packet so that she thought she was crossing the rift on her own, and so that she'd forgotten the part where we'd already crashed."

"The nanobots," I said, trying to piece what she was saying together. "You made me sabotage my own ship. I thought I was bringing back a shell, but it was a machine."

"Yes, but it wasn't really sabotage, was it? The nanobots I had you plant simply created the impression of a dangerous situation, which you quickly solved."

"So the power surge wasn't real?"

"Not exactly, no. It just appeared to be so. But to your question: Clare never knew that she was acting out my program; in fact, most of the time she was just being Clare. She really is a good girl, and you two make a great team."

"But she did know," I said. "She had these moments where she felt like something wasn't right. It scared her."

"Interesting. I didn't anticipate that, but I am just a subservient machine myself. Only as advanced as the creatures who made me."

"What happens to her now?"

"Clare? Oh, I'll wipe this whole sequence from her virtual memory. She's already been reinserted into the simulation—that is, until her rescue is complete."

"And what happens to me?"

"Well, now we come to the whole reason I brought you here, Will. I am hoping that you'll help me save Clare and her family."

"How am I going to do that?"

"Actually, I've already trained you in what to do. I simply need you to perform the polarity reversal that you were planning to do with Clare. Resetting just a few key circuit systems should allow me to finally reboot the ship's engines and get the *Derelict* back online."

"Why didn't you just do that yourself?"

Alina made a sound like a sigh. "It's funny. Despite all my functions and capabilities, rewiring the circuit boards requires the one thing I don't have: a body. Specifically, hands."

"Then why didn't you just have Clare do it, or one of her family?" I said, motioning to them—

But as I did, my vision swam, and a hot flash of dizziness washed over me. I glanced at my communicator and saw that the treatment Judy had given me was at 82 percent. The treatment she'd designed to remove metals from my system... were those metals the nanobots? I blinked away the woozy feeling and glanced at Clare's body in the pod again—

And nearly screamed.

Clare's face had changed. It was no longer her peaceful, sleeping self. Her cheeks looked sunken, the skin stretched and gray. There were holes by her temples, pits on her neck, and her eyes were hollowed-out black sockets. The rest of her family, too; all their faces looked like corpses—

Then normal again. I blinked and it was back to Clare, just like I remembered her...but my heart was still pounding. Had that been real?

"I didn't know the solution to resetting the circuits until you figured it out," Alina was saying. "And I no longer have enough power left even to wake Clare and her family to do it."

Another stab of pain in my head, a shudder—the faces in the pods flashed again: Clare, her parents, her brother, all of them like mummies, skin like ancient paper, bone and teeth pushing through—

"Will?"

I blinked hard, tried to slow my breathing. The faces were normal again.

"Sure, yeah, that makes sense," I said, but I was stalling now. My brain felt like mud, and *nothing* made sense. Those dead faces echoed behind my eyes. Why was I seeing that?

But maybe I knew. Ever since I'd started Judy's

treatment, I'd been seeing Clare less. She'd disappeared those times. If the treatment was removing the nanobots from my system, maybe now I was seeing—

Less of what Alina wants me to see. The thought hit me like a gravity well. Judy…she hadn't actually seen Clare; none of them had, until—*until they were infected, too.* I remembered now: They'd all been sniffling with cold symptoms like mine. The allergic reaction that meant the nanobots were inside them, too. And what had Judy's note said about the medicine? *Writing this down before I forget*…Almost like she *knew* there was something wrong with her.

"Will, are you feeling all right?"

I snapped out of my thoughts. "Yeah, I'm okay, sorry. This is just a lot. Um, if I'm going to restart your ship, I need those batteries I told Clare about."

"Yes, I have already identified the location of the correct supply closet. It will appear on that panel that is now lighting up to your left."

A square on the floor, which was actually the

wall, lit up. I turned to it, but as I did, I felt another hot flash in my head, my neck burned, and I glanced at the pods. Clare looked ancient again, like a zombie—

They're dead, I thought, a freezing certainty coursing through me. *Or at least, their bodies are. They've been like this for thousands of years. And: Alina is lying about being able to save them....No matter how much power she had, they are too far decayed to ever be awakened.* But then why lie? Suddenly, a new certainty flooded through me: *Alina doesn't know I know. She doesn't know that Judy's treatment is working and that I can see through her lies. At least not yet.*

And I knew I had to keep it that way. "This panel here?" I said, crouching and running my fingers over the map.

"Yes, can you decipher it?"

"I think so." Except I was barely looking at it. "This is where we are?" I said, tapping a dot.

"Yes, and that red dot is where the panels are. Two corridors away."

"Okay..." I traced my finger over the route, slowly, to buy myself more time to think.

So first, Alina had infected me, and then, when the rest of my family tried to stop me from coming here—they'd known Clare wasn't real, even shown me the proof on Penny's video and the security cameras—she'd infected them, too. That made sense, but it still felt like there was something I was missing, a shadow in my thoughts.

"Will, do you see where to go? It's time to get moving."

"I think so." I turned and looked at the pods. Clare's long-dead face...it was all I could see now; the spell had worn off completely. I checked my communicator and saw that my treatment had reached 90 percent. I stood, starting to shake, but I couldn't let Alina see. "And once I fix the circuits, you can restart your engines, and then...that's it? You leave?"

"That's correct. Off we go."

The mummified skin, in all four pods...

"And then you can just wake them up?" I managed to say, but at the same time my mind was racing. Alina had described what happened next a little bit differently before; this time she'd said *off we go*, but last time she'd said *until her rescue is complete*. But you couldn't rescue Clare and her family. These bodies could never be woken up. In order to rescue them, you would need—

"Oh, Will, stop stalling."

"I'm not stalling, I—"

"You figured it out, is that it?"

"I didn't—"

I stopped because a sound was reaching my ears from somewhere in the ship. A rhythmic banging, gentle, but steady. Getting louder.

"I had my suspicions, of course," said Alina. "Don't you think I could tell that I was losing my link with your nanobots? Nice job, trying to conceal that, by the way. You really are a sharp mind."

"What are you talking about?" I said.

That clanging sound grew louder.

"I think you know."

Lights flashed in the doorway overhead. Shuffling, rustling sounds, now legs swung over the edge, and a person in a space suit appeared—a suit just like mine. The figure dropped down on a safety line into the compartment.

"Hey, Will," said Judy.

Dad dropped down next.

"What are you guys doing here?" I shouted. "You have to get out!"

"Get out?" Mom had lowered beside Dad, a smile on her face. "Why would we do that?"

I waved my hands at the pods. "Because it's a trap!"

But Dad and Judy just shared a look.

"What's he talking about?" said Dad.

"Not sure," said Mom.

"Guys—" I shouted.

But Mom talked right over me. "Alina, what did you want us to do next?"

"First things first," said Alina. "Grab your son."

CHAPTER

13

K eep moving," Judy said, shoving my back.

"Judy," I pleaded, halfway up the safety line out of the lab. "She's controlling you. This isn't—"

"Don't listen to him, Judy," said Alina. "You know that you and your family are doing a great service."

"Okay, I won't," Judy replied, her face blank.

"They're going to steal our bodies!" I said, because now I understood what Alina truly wanted. "She's going to download Clare's family *into* us! That's what she means by a *rescue*."

"Will," Judy said in her stern doctor's voice, "you are not making sense right now."

"Yeah, that's ridiculous," said Dad, who was

crouched outside the hatch. He reached down and yanked me up out of the compartment. Judy climbed out behind me and the two grabbed me by the arms.

"Guys! Don't do this!"

"Mom," Judy said, looking back into the lab. "Get yourself prepped for the transfer."

"No, don't!" I shouted. "The transfer is going to kill you guys!"

"Will, come on," said Mom, grinning. "Alina says we're getting uploaded into a fascinating simulation. She says she can cater it to our every whim."

"Yeah," said Dad, "it's going to be a thousand times better than this watery dump we've been living on."

"Can't wait," Judy agreed, smiling.

"You *GUYS!*" I shouted, struggling against their grip. "You have to listen to me! She's controlling your minds with nanotech! That's what my rash was from! These colds you have are an allergic reaction—"

"Will," Judy said, her face darkening. "You've

always been smart, but I've told you before: I don't do science fiction."

Dad and Judy dragged me down the hall, and after a few useless minutes, I stopped fighting and just stumbled along through branching corridors until we reached the hatch to the engine room.

Inside, they pushed me against the circular railing. My headlamp reflected on the giant engine coil that had been glowing so brightly when I'd first seen this room with Clare. It was dark now, crusted with corrosion and dripping with rusty water.

"This one over here," said Dad, opening a panel in the wall.

"Here are the batteries." Judy removed a black equipment bag from her shoulder and tossed it at my feet.

"You brought *our* batteries?" I said.

"You see the corrosion on these walls?" said Dad. "Imagine what four thousand years of that did to their batteries. Now, hurry up. We need time to shave our heads for the transfer."

"Dad!" I pleaded. Couldn't they *hear* themselves?

"Will, stop fighting this," Alina said pleasantly over the ship's comms. "I promise I'm going to take good care of you. Now, attach the batteries to the fourth circuit panel on the left."

"No," I said. "I'm not going to help you."

"I understand that you might feel this way," said Alina, "but I should be clear: I have you, and I'm going to use your bodies either way. If you would like to live on past this moment, I would suggest that you do what I say."

I had no response. All my hope was draining out of me. I glanced at Judy's and Dad's blank faces, and then knelt beside the panel, my fingers shaking, tugged out the circuit, and laid it on the floor, which was actually the wall. But at the same time, I yelled at myself: *Think!* There had to be something I could do to get out of this, to break the spell.

"Get to it, William," said Judy. "We don't have all day."

I took out the first battery, tightened the wires,

and then held it over the board, running my fingers over the light tubes. "Sorry," I said quickly, "it will just take a sec."

I attached the first battery to the circuit board, then chained the rest of them in a line. When they were all arranged, I ran a wire back to the board. "Okay," I said, "this should reverse the polarity and allow the ship to come back online." I connected the wire to the board.

There was a little buzz of energy, and then a small light grew inside one of the thin glass tubes on the circuit board and began to pulse. More lights ignited, and still more, spreading across the board and then jumping up to the other circuit boards in the panel. Lights bloomed into more lights, the ship coming back to life. Now a rumble of machinery in the floor and a burst of air through vents around the room.

"You did it, Will," said Alina, like a proud parent. "I knew I could count on you. Now, I will be gone briefly as I reboot my core systems, but I'm leaving you in good hands."

"We're on it," said Judy. "Okay, Will, on your feet. Let's get back to the—"

A harsh sound cut through the silence: a siren blaring in pulsing tones that echoed through the corridors, louder than the rumbling floors.

"What *is* that?" Dad said, wincing and turning to the door. "It sounds like it's right outside."

"Will?" said Judy, peering at me suspiciously.

I held up my hands. "I didn't do anything!"

Dad stepped out into the corridor. "It's here," he called from around the corner. "Looks like a faulty sensor of some kind, like a fire detector. Alina! Can you turn it off?"

"She's still busy rebooting," said Judy.

"It looks like if I hoist you up, you could deactivate it," said Dad.

Judy glanced at me and I just shrugged. "Where exactly am I going to go?" She nodded and joined Dad.

With the alarm blaring, I knelt there, still trying to think of anything I could do to stop this from happening—

"Will!"

I heard a voice like a hissing whisper, barely audible over the alarm.

"Down here."

I glanced to my side and spied one of those comms panels by my knee. A little light was blinking there. Was that—

"Clare?" I whispered, adrenaline surging through me—but at the same time I thought, *No*, this was probably just another a trick....

"It's me," Clare's voice said from the little speaker grate on the panel, the tiny yellow light beside it flashing as she spoke. "I escaped the simulation. Well, I had help from my family."

"How is that possible?"

"Shh! No time for that. Did my distraction work?"

I glanced toward the hall and then lowered my head right by the panel. "Yeah, nice job."

"Thanks. Alina placed me back in the simulation but hasn't erased my memory yet. What she's done...Will, I'm so sorry. You have to believe me: I had no idea what was really going on—"

"I believe you," I whispered. "But how are you outside? Or, in there, in the wall?"

"My dad helped me download myself into the system's online RAM. It's...it's weird not to have a body, but I guess I haven't actually had one for a long time."

"You're *in* the ship's systems? But why?"

"So I can help you. Now, listen, quick. I'm going to display a code on this screen. Take a photo of it."

A series of symbols appeared on the comm panel, in Clare's language. "How are you doing that?" I asked.

"Just kind of spreading myself out there," she said. "It feels weird, like I'm part of all this programming, sort of like I'm swimming in it.... This is what I've been all along; I just didn't know."

"I'm sorry."

"Don't be. Did you get the code yet?"

I held my communicator over the screen and snapped a picture. "Got it. What is this?"

"That's the passcode to reset the ship's central computer. That will completely reboot Alina to her factory settings."

"Okay. But…" A chill passed through me. "Won't that also reboot everything else, including the virtual storage?"

"Nope. The virtual storage and other hard drives will remain intact. My family will be fine."

"What about the ship's RAM? The part you're in."

Clare didn't respond right away. "You'll know the ship is online when the engine core starts to spin. As soon as it does, put that code into the keypad on your terminal. You see it there?"

The side of the comms panel had two lines of symbols, perhaps to be used like a keyboard. "Yeah, I see it."

"Okay, after you enter the code, hold the last symbol for five seconds. The reboot will start. And once it does you have to get out of there."

"Out of the engine room?"

"No, off the ship completely."

"But my family is all under Alina's control."

"The reboot sequence will cut Alina's connection to them."

"Why do we need to get off the ship?"

"Because I'm going to launch it," said Clare. "I should be able to initiate the sequence as soon as the reboot begins."

"Launch the ship? How? Aren't you out of fuel?"

"We lost our electronics; we never lost our fuel. We've been sitting on nearly full tanks ever since we got stuck in the rift; we just couldn't use them."

"Okay, but how do we get out? Me and my family."

"There's an escape pod right off the med lab. Launching it should get you to the surface, and out of our way."

The siren in the hall cut off.

"Man," said Dad, "that's the loudest concert I've ever been to."

"They're coming back," I said to the speaker.

"Okay," said Clare. "Just like we planned. Trust me!"

"Wait, you didn't say what will happen to *you* if we reboot."

But Clare didn't answer because just then, Judy and Dad stepped back into the compartment. As they did, another wave of rumbling shook the ship.

Bright lights flashed behind me, and I turned to see the engine core coming to life and beginning to spin in a figure eight pattern, glowing a shimmering white.

"Excellent work," said Dad.

"Alina will be pleased," said Judy.

"Good," I lied. "Just, uh, one more thing, here…" I tapped my communicator, brought up the photo of the code, then started tapping the symbols into the comms panel. As I touched each one, it appeared on-screen.

"Come on, Will, get up," Judy said, stepping toward me. "Hey, what are you doing?"

"Nothing." Just a couple more—

Judy grabbed my arm. "Hey!" she shouted. "Dad! He's doing something!"

Both of them lunged toward me. One more symbol to tap in—but they both grabbed me by the arms and dragged me away just before my finger could hit the key.

"No!" I shouted, writhing against their grip, but it was no use.

"Come on, Will!" Dad shouted in my ear, and he sounded as furious, as unlike my dad as he ever had. "Enough! The work is done. We're going back."

They hauled me out of the compartment, my feet scrambling on the floor. "Stop!" I shouted, fresh tears coming to my eyes. "She's going to kill us! You don't understand—"

"We understand that you need to shut *up*," Judy hissed, her grip tightening.

"No, please!" My feet bumped the doorway and then we were back out in the hall. I lost sight of the control panel, those symbols still flashing, one left to go. Clare waiting for me—we were doomed. All of us.

"This is how it has to go," Dad was saying as we emerged in the corridor. "Everything will be fine soon—"

Suddenly, there was a dull thud. Dad made a gasping sound, and his grip released from my arm. Judy and I toppled sideways, off balance. I wrenched myself free of her and spun, slamming into the wall. I looked up to see Dad lying in a heap on the floor, and standing above him—

It was Dr. Smith. Breathing hard and holding one of the lengths of pipe that we'd thought were driftwood. "I hope I didn't break anything," she said, looking down at Dad. Then to me. "Hi, Will. Oh, hey, look out!" She nodded behind me.

"You!" Judy was lunging past me, at Dr. Smith. I thought to stick out my foot, and sent her crashing to the floor.

Smith leaped down on top of her, pinning her to the ground with her knees and then shoving the pipe down against her neck.

"Don't hurt her!" I shouted instinctively.

"Relax, William. I've had more experience than you might think with hurting people. I also know how to keep them right where I want them." She pressed the pipe down, holding Judy in place. "Now, I hope this little lifesaving effort by me can help us move past our differences and establish a working relationship based on trust and—"

"What are you doing here?" I said, pushing away

from the wall and getting my balance. "Why aren't you like *them*?"

"So many reasons," said Dr. Smith, glancing at me with a smile. "You should ask my therapist. Oh, except I guess that's me. But really, it's so simple. I was in the airlock the whole time. And after I saw you walking around all green-snotted and raving about some imaginary girl, with Judy talking about allergic reactions, I wasn't about to complain. If there's one thing I've always had, it's a good survival instinct."

"Why didn't you tell them if you were suspicious?" I shouted.

"Well," said Dr. Smith, "I may have excellent instincts, but *sharing* has never been my strong suit. Besides, look how it turned out. After your genius of a sister here managed to unlock my door, I watched your whole family march off like good little zombies, then followed them out here to that hatch in the middle of the ocean. I wasn't sure what to do, but when the ship started to rumble like it was turning on, I figured I'd better get down here, because I am not missing my ride off this place."

"It's not a ride!" I said. "The ship is trying to steal our bodies to rescue its crew."

Dr. Smith's face fell. "Oh, that's unfortunate. Do you have a plan to stop that?"

"Actually"—I darted for the compartment door—"I do."

I lunged back to the comm panel on the floor, sliding on my knees, and tapped the last symbol, holding it down for five seconds.

All the lights in the room flashed back to red. For a moment, the rumbling of machinery and the whir of fans paused in total silence—then the quiet was pierced by a shrieking sound like when a microphone feeds back.

"WHAT HAVE YOU DONE?" Alina roared, her voice flooding the room. "YOU CAN'T—" And then she was cut off by her own voice, speaking a calm, generic command: "System reboot initiated. Please back up all perishable files."

I jumped to my feet and ran back into the corridor. "Okay, that's it!"

Judy flinched beneath Dr. Smith's grip. "What's happening?" Her eyes darted around. "Where are we?"

"They're okay now," I said to Smith. "Let her go."

Smith looked from Judy to me and back. I could see her working through whatever devious thoughts she had—but she got to her feet, releasing Judy.

"Quick," I said, kneeling beside Judy and slipping off my pack. "We have to start their treatment." I pulled out two of the space needles and handed one to Smith. "Give that one to my dad."

As Smith turned, I stuck the green pod into the port on Judy's sleeve. She flinched. "What are you—" But when she saw the needle, her eyes widened with recognition. I pressed the INITIATE command.

Judy shook her head with a confused, exhausted look. "Will…" She blinked. "What's going on?"

"Yeah." Dad groaned. He rolled over onto his side, and I felt a surge of relief to see that Smith had actually done what I'd asked and given him the medicine. "What is this place?"

"We're in a different spaceship," I said, jumping to my feet and pulling Judy up. "You guys have been…well, you haven't been yourselves. I can explain more later."

"I feel like there was someone talking in my head and now they're gone." Judy rubbed her fingers over the space needle on her arm. "I made these, didn't I? I found the…"

"The titanium silicate compound," I said. "You figured out my allergic reaction. It's what this ship's nanotechnology is made of."

"I did—oh, ow." She rubbed at her helmet. "Something was infecting all of us. It had been controlling you; that's what I'd figured out, but then…"

"Then it took control of you, too," I said. "But you made this medicine first. Once I started using it, it broke the ship's hold on me."

Judy nodded. "Chelation treatment. It's used to filter metals from the blood."

"What's *she* doing here?" Dad said, noticing Smith standing nearby.

"Nice to see you, too, John," said Smith. "I just stopped by to save you all from yourselves, *again*."

"You—" Dad started, his face darkening.

"She's telling the truth," I said. "This time."

Dad looked around. "Where are Mom and Penny?"

"Mom's in the med lab," I said.

"Penny is lying unconscious in the *Jupiter*," Smith reported. When all our gazes snapped to her, she quickly added, "Not my fault! When the rest of you lined up and left like little lemmings, she and Don just slumped to the floor."

"Alina only needs four of us to match Clare's family," I said.

"Go, Will!" Clare's voice erupted from a comm panel on the wall near us. "You have to hurry! I'm starting the launch sequence!"

"Launch?" Judy's eyes snapped to the speaker. "Who—"

"That was Clare, and we need to get back to the lab right now."

"System reboot complete" said the calm version of Alina's voice. "Automated launch sequence initiated."

The entire floor began to shake.

The *Derelict's* engine core shrieked and began to spin faster, throwing off sparks and a molten orange glow that was brightening by the second.

"Come on!" I said. "We have to move."

"Yeah," said Judy, "that's probably a good idea."

CHAPTER

14

We stumbled down the corridor. Dad staggered, losing his balance.

"Why does my head hurt?"

"I hit you with a pipe," said Smith.

Dad glanced at her. "Oh."

"Here," I said as we reached the hatch to the med lab. I gathered the safety line from the floor, hooked in, and started down into the lab, Judy right behind me.

"What's happening?" Mom called weakly from below. I got my feet to the floor and turned to see her lying across the top of two of the pods.

"Don't look underneath you," I warned, but I should have known better, because that made Mom do exactly that. She rolled over to see the decaying face of one of Clare's parents. "Oh!" She recoiled and tumbled to the floor.

"On the bright side," I said, rushing over and holding my hand out to her, "you didn't shave your head."

"I was going to *what?*" said Mom.

"Just take this," I said, slinging my backpack around and handing her a space needle.

"Will, to your right!" said Clare, her voice coming through another comm panel on the floor of the lab. A yellow light had lit above a small hatch, and the door slid open.

I pointed Judy toward it. "We have to get everyone in there."

Judy just nodded. She'd been staring at the pods, her face tight and her eyes wide, and she had to tear her gaze away.

Dad's boots hit the floor, and he looked at the pods in the same way.

"John!" Mom rushed over to him. "Are you okay?"

"I'm good," he said. "Mostly. You?"

"I don't know." Mom looked at me. "Will...I think we owe you an apology."

"Let's just get out of here first." I motioned to the hatch, but then my eyes darted around the room. "Wait. Where's Smith?"

Dad looked up to the doorway we'd lowered through. "Smith?"

No answer.

"Maybe she's hurt," Dad said.

"No." I thought of what she'd said when she saved me. *I am not missing my ride off this place.* "She's going to try to leave with the ship."

"Will, one of your people is heading for the cockpit," said Clare. "We don't have the energy to turn on all the life support systems for launch. She's going to die if she comes with us."

I saw Mom and Dad share a look.

Dad sighed and grabbed the safety line. "Where's the cockpit?"

"Clare, can you light the way?" I asked.

"Yes, but you have to hurry!"

"What else is new?" said Dad, and he retracted the safety line and zipped up out of sight.

"John!" Mom shouted. "Be careful!"

"Let's get to the pod," I said, tugging Mom's arm.

She nodded but stumbled as she started that way. "I'm still so woozy," she said, and slumped against me.

Judy rushed over, and we guided Mom through the hatch.

We found ourselves in a tiny escape pod with three rows of seats, aimed toward the ocean surface. Above the front row of seats was a cockpit window that seemed to be looking out into solid sand. The lights on the console were blinking to life.

Judy and I guided Mom to a seat and buckled her in, her head lolling back.

"Thanks," she whispered faintly, and then her eyes fluttered shut.

Judy climbed up to one of the top two seats, in front of the controls.

I went back to the hatch. "Dad?" I called.

No answer. The rumbling of the ship, the blowing of the vents, the blinking of the lights: They were all getting more intense.

"Will, you need to get safely aboard," said Clare.

"I know." I stood there gripping the hatchway, shaking. "DAD!"

"Will, anything?" said Judy.

"No…"

Something flashed in the med lab. A glint of movement. The safety line! Now a shadow and a figure tumbled down through the door and snapped tight at the end of the safety line, hanging there limply. Smith! She lowered in a heap to the floor, and a moment later, Dad was sliding down and landing beside her.

"Dad!" I raced over to him.

"Now we're even," he said, grabbing the unconscious Smith by the arm. "Help me get her."

We hoisted her up by the shoulders and dragged her into the pod, dumping her in a seat beside Mom.

"Time to go, people!" Judy shouted.

Everything around us was rattling and vibrating. Dad buckled himself in. "Whoa," he said, "I do not feel so good."

I started to climb up to the seat beside Judy—but instead darted over to the hatch and looked back out into the med lab.

"Come on, Will!" said Judy.

"One sec!" I gazed at the row of pods, at the silhouette of a face inside the nearest one: Clare, the girl I'd known but never known—

"Will, are you out of there yet?" the virtual Clare called from the comms.

"Almost," I said. "Just, um, I guess this is goodbye, huh?"

"Not yet," she said. "Now, buckle up, already!"

I shut the hatch and climbed to the seat beside Judy, who was gazing at the controls. Looking behind me, I saw that Dad had passed out now, too.

"Are we supposed to have any clue how to fly this thing?" Judy said.

The rumbling increased, becoming almost deafening. There was a hiss, and I saw streams of bubbles flowing over the cockpit window above us. Columns of sand cracked apart and water gushed in, making swirling clouds of sand and bubbles, and now distant light filtered down from somewhere far above.

I scanned the controls. "I'm no pilot," I said, pointing to a large yellow-lit button, "but I bet we press that."

"Good guess," said Judy, and she slammed her palm against it. Red lights flashed inside the pod, and there was a giant *clunk!* The pod jolted and the rumbling from the ship ceased. We'd separated from it, and it felt like we were floating, everything getting weirdly quiet.

"Okay, now what?" Judy asked.

A hum started to grow in the quiet, then became a roar, and then we were shoved back against our seats as the pod shot upward. Sand and bubbles blurred across the cockpit window.

"I guess there's autopilot," I said.

"Aah, my ears." Judy pressed her hands against her helmet. I felt it, too, a heavy sensation in my head as my suit fought to compensate.

The light got brighter above us and suddenly the pod burst out of the water, was airborne for a moment, then crashed back down and floated on the waves.

I sat there for a second, catching my breath. Judy was doing the same. I never thought I could be so glad to see the clouds of this world over our heads.

As the water sheeted off the cockpit, I spotted the *Jupiter* and our little island not far in the distance.

Right beside us, though, the sea was starting to boil.

"We should get to shore," I said.

"Agreed," said Judy. She surveyed the controls and settled on a little lever. When she pushed it forward, the pod churned through the water, but almost immediately beached on the sand, just off the edge of our island. Waves started to lash against us from behind, knocking us sideways. Judy tossed off her restraints. "Everybody out. Quick!"

"This way," I said, noticing there was another hatch on the starboard side of the pod, which was now facing the island as the waves crashed into the port side. Judy and I strained to carry Dad out and laid him on the sand up out of the reach of the waves. Then we went back for Mom and did the same, and finally Dr. Smith. All of them muttered incoherently, their eyes fluttering.

I turned back to the pod, but just then a huge wave broke over the top of it, rolled it forward, and then sucked it back into deeper water. The open hatch became a waterfall, and the pod started to submerge. Behind it, the ocean bubbled and frothed.

The ground began to shake, and a deep rumbling grew. Jets of water shot up into the air, hundreds of meters tall.

Judy and I stumbled to keep our balance as the massive nose of the *Derelict* rose from the surface, streams of water and sand cascading off it. Those three triangle pylons that I'd mistaken for rocks looked insignificant compared to the true size of the ship. Its once sleek surface was streaked with corrosion.

Water sprayed against our visors, wind buffeted us, waves sloshed over our island. The enormous ship thrust out of the water, its sides towering over us and its brilliant, blazing engine burning free of the ocean in tumbling clouds of smoke and mist.

"I can't believe that thing was right there," said Judy.

I shielded my eyes and watched as the *Derelict* climbed and climbed, trailing exhaust behind it, water still streaming from its sides. It breached the clouds overhead, and then, almost immediately, it was completely lost from sight. The roar from its engine still vibrated our chests, and the waves from its departure rampaged about.

In another moment, the sound had faded, too. The waves were already calming.

I kept watching the clouds. The smoke trail from the engine had nearly dissipated. And I felt a lump forming in my throat.

Another friend, lost.

"Will." Judy elbowed me gently and pointed toward the bluff beside Mom's office.

Standing just beyond, on the Whaleback, was Clare, waving to us.

"You see that?" I said to Judy.

"I do." She glanced at the sky. "Hurry. I bet she doesn't have long."

I broke into a sprint across the sand, boots splashing. I could see Clare grinning, but when I got close, I also saw that her eyes were overflowing with tears. I stopped in front of her, breathless, and saw, too, that the waves and rocks were visible *through* her. She was a transmission again, like she'd been the first time I'd met her.

"Hey," she said, sniffling.

"Hi."

"Don't worry," she said, motioning to herself. "I'm not in your mind. I am broadcasting myself through the ship's holographic transmitter—" Just then a static line rippled through her and she winked out and returned. "Range is weakening. We're moving out of the atmosphere."

"How long do you have until you're—"

"Erased?" Clare hitched, like she was holding

back a sob. "The system reboot will hit the main computer's RAM in"—she glitched—"seconds."

"How long?"

"It doesn't matter." Clare sniffled and did her best to smile. "My parents and brother are safe in the virtual storage. I set the ship's course for Antares, so if we ever get found, sometime in the future, who knows? Maybe there will be a way to save them. And they can warn everyone about the Antares supernova ahead of time. Maybe it will even be the future version of us that finds the *Derelict*—"

"Clare," I said. "What about saving you?"

Clare shook her head. "It's okay. They're safe. You're safe."

"But—"

"I just wanted to say goodbye. I'm going to miss you." Clare rolled her tear-filled eyes. "Well, technically I guess I won't be missing anything soon, but, I mean—"

"I'll miss you, too," I said, and now my eyes were

also welling up, my whole body feeling like it was being squeezed tight. "I wish you didn't have to go."

Clare sighed. "So do I."

A big feeling broke like a wave in me, and I balled my fists and wanted to scream. Why did things have to end? Why did friends have to leave you? Why couldn't the good things keep going on, being good, the way they always were right before you realized *how* good they were? Right before you understood that they couldn't last....

Clare's hand moved over my shoulder like she was trying to pat it. I thought I felt a little tingle of electricity there, as her fingers flitted through my suit, but it was probably my imagination.

"It's okay, Will," she said. "I hope you find a new fort."

I held back my tears. "Yeah."

"Don't forget to hang the moss. Use the—" She glitched out again. *One...two...* My breath caught in my throat. The wind blew steadily, the waves sloshing. Was that it?

Then Clare was back. We just looked at each other. What could you possibly say in the last moment you were ever going to see someone? In the last moment when they would ever even *be*? Another second passed. *Think!* I shouted at myself.

"Almost time to go," she said.

"I know." And then I stepped forward and wrapped my arms around her. I put my head by her shoulder and closed my eyes. Even though Clare wasn't really there, even though she was just a brief wave of light, a memory...she was real to me, she—

"Bye, Will."

The air between my arms sizzled. I opened my eyes.

Only wind, and sand, and water. I looked to the sky. Only clouds.

"Bye," I whispered.

I stood there for a minute, hating everything. This stupid planet, that stupid AI, the stupid universe that took everything away...

I turned toward the *Jupiter*. Judy was standing by our parents, waving for me to come back.

Well, it hadn't taken everything. Not yet, anyway.

"You okay?" she asked as I trudged back to her.

I just shrugged. "Not really."

She put an arm around me. "Come on, we have to get everyone inside. They're all going to have quite the headache when they wake up."

"Do you think they'll remember what happened?"

"We'll see. I...sort of remember? The stuff before you broke the spell is really foggy. But even after that..." She glanced out to sea, and then to the sky. "Were we really on that ship? Did all that really happen?"

Did it? The thought was like a spear of ice. *Yes*, I told myself. *It may be over now, but it's in my memories. Just as real as the Robot.* "It happened."

"I'm sorry I didn't believe you about Clare," said Judy. "If I had listened, if I'd taken what you were saying seriously, this might never have happened."

"There was a giant ship with a desperate AI

buried right near our *Jupiter*," I said. "This was all probably going to happen at some point."

"Well, then I'm glad it happened to you," said Judy.

"Thanks."

"No, I mean it. Clare saved our lives because of *you*. Just like the Robot saved our lives multiple times—he dragged me out of that ice—because of you, Will Robinson. Apparently, you're the best friend in the universe."

The words warmed me, and I raised my eyebrows at her. "Thanks."

Judy looked past me to the sandbars I'd explored. "Maybe during the next round of spring tides, you can take me exploring with you."

"Could we build a fort?"

"Only if I get to sit in it and quietly read my medical books."

I smiled. "Sounds like a plan."

Judy knelt beside Mom, Dad, and Dr. Smith, and started checking their vitals.

I turned and looked back out across the sand